MW00461618

HER HOT DOCTOR

GRACE DEVON

Copyright © 2016 All Rights Reserved

All rights reserved. No part of this publication may be reproduced, distributed, or transmitted in any form or by any means, including photocopying, recording, or other electronic or mechanical methods, without the prior written permission of the publisher, except in the case of brief quotations embodied in critical reviews and certain other noncommercial uses permitted by copyright law.

Dear Reader,

Thank you for checking out "Her Hot Doctor". I hope that you enjoy getting to know Zeb and Cassidy! Zeb surprised me as I wrote, and I learned that he had a lot to share, as did Cassidy. They filled in each other's empty spaces, and I am glad that they found each other. I hope that you enjoy their rollercoaster ride -- it is full of ups and downs, and they each learn a lot about themselves along the ride!

I worked on a busy Medical Surgical floor for years as a nurse, and now enjoy crafting stories for you to enjoy. While certain medical settings and types of doctors are close to my heart, I am also open to new settings and heroes. If you have a certain kind of crush-worthy-doctor that you'd love to read about in mind, please reach out through email (gacedevon333@gmail.com). I love to write the stories that you enjoy reading. I look forward to hearing from you soon! Enjoy this story about Cassidy Novotny and her relationship with her gifted, smokin' hot doctor, Zeb Morgan.

If you enjoy getting to know the doctors at Baily Mills, be sure to check out Jack and Danielle's story, "Her Chief Resident"!

Love! Grace

TABLE OF CONTENTS

ONE

Zeb was glad that he had followed the black Cadillac with tinted windows. Although the thug who'd come to his door wasn't Darrious, it was Darrious' errand boy, and that was enough for Zeb. Thankfully, despite his anger, he'd had enough clarity to grab his passport.

He wouldn't need it to get into Canada, but sometimes on the way back into the US, having it on hand helped to expedite the process.

And he wanted to expedite the process.

He wanted to spend as little time on this bullshit as possible.

In and out, he thought. *One-two punch. Over and done with.*

Deliver the message: You're not messing with me anymore.

"What is the reason for your visit into Canada this evening, Mr. Morgan?"

"Doctor Morgan," Zeb corrected the border control officer out of sheer habit. Due to his age, people never seemed to get it right away that he was a doctor. His renegade spiky blonde hair and rough good looks made him look more like a Calvin Klein underwear model than a doctor. He usually had to spell it out. But not to border control. "Sorry," he corrected himself. "I'm visiting an old friend."

An old friend; yeah right. 'Friend' was the opposite of what Darrious was.

Once through border control, the road was clear and Zeb pushed the speed limit. His bike was running smoothly and the October air's biting chill in the places that it crept through his leather outerwear made him feel alert. He wanted to make good time. What with the intensity of the sixth year OR schedule in addition to nights on call, he'd almost been tempted to let this one lie. Just to pay up.

But his moral code rebuked. He was tired of paying the blackmail fees that Darrious enforced quarterly. It wasn't right. He shouldn't have to keep paying for the mistake he'd made ten years ago.

He'd been trying to find dirt on Darrious for years, and finally he'd gotten something.

He'd set a mousetrap, and caught the mouse.

The lights of Montreal grew in the distance. Pinpoint dots of orange, gold and soft pink came into focus and became streetlamps and apartment windows.

It was almost ten pm when the black SUV slowed and turned down an alleyway in the heart of the New City. Zeb knew this must be the end of the line. The errand boy must be delivering his collections to Darrious, the boss with hands in all kinds of pies -- some of them rotten.

Zeb pulled to the side of the road and parked. He jumped off of his bike, removed his helmet, and hurried to the corner. He looked down the alley just in time to see a glimpse of the thug disappearing behind a nondescript door into a large windowless building.

Zeb walked down the cluttered, narrow alley, looking both ways as he walked. He seemed to be in a somewhat seedy part of town. He zipped his leather jacket collar up, guarding against a gust of wind that whipped stray wrappers and papers into the air and sent an empty can rolling and rattling against the pavement.

Zeb knew that Darrious, not much older than himself, had married a year ago. Zeb did not want to be the one to break up a marriage, but he also didn't want to see Darrious get away with cheating on his wife.

He knew that if he could get some pictures of Darrious and his new mistress, it might be enough to scare Darrious into leaving him alone. *Two can play this game*, he thought.

The door was heavy but unlocked, and once he pulled it open a thudding bass hit him in the chest, vibrating into his very bones. The hallway was dark. He was in a back entryway, and he saw doors to his left that looked like a mix of offices and storage areas. The floor was bare cement, and cases of beverages lined the walls.

This was as far as he'd gotten, in his mind when he had worked over his plan. He knew the thug would lead him to Darrious, and he hoped that Darrious would spend time with his mistress, and that he could catch some incriminating evidence on camera.

Now he had to wait and see if the woman was here.

She must be, thought Zeb, hoping that he hadn't taken the trip for nothing. He reviewed the facts. Darrious' wife was away for the weekend. If Zeb knew Darrious, and he felt he did after ten years, he knew the guy would be taking is mistress home with him tonight.

Only Zeb didn't know where Darrious lived. He'd have to follow him. This was more than he wanted to do, but if it put an end to the blackmail, it was well worth enduring the sleaziness of it all.

He'd have to wait until his blackmailer left for the evening in order to get even. He'd get even, and then he'd be free.

He was ready to put his past behind him.

He walked towards the bar, hoping it wouldn't be a long wait.

Places like this reminded him of a person he no longer wanted to be.

Two

Cassidy leaned into Margo, letting her cheek press up against her friend's as the flash went off. Done with the mini photo shoot at last, she looked at Margo and straightened the plastic silver tiara that was on Margo's head.

"There," she said, with a smile. "Your tiara is perfect." Cassidy admired the little shimmering pink gemstones embedded in the silver plastic. It was actually quite beautiful.

Margo smiled, and pulled the crown off of her head. She placed it on Cassidy's.

"Trade you," Margo said, pulling on the pink feather boa that Cassidy wore and then wrapping it around her own neck. "I like this thing. The feathers are so soft! And the color... it's the brightest pink I think I've ever seen. Beck, good job with the party favors girl." Margo, the bride, gave Becky a smile.

The limo rolled to a stop. The music that pumped through the limo's speakers was loud and Margo was clearly excited about arriving at the club. She started dancing along to the song that was playing before opening the door, twirling the tips of her hot pink feather boa in circles and shimmying her shoulders.

"I hope you like this!" Becky squealed and started dancing too. Although Cassidy was the maid of honor, Becky had taken on the duty of planning the bachelorette party due to Cassidy's recent condition. The mysterious, annoying symptoms that had been haunting her for the last year had recently ramped up in just the past three months, when she started noticing the blood.

But her gynecologist hadn't had any answers about the blood in her urine, nor the cramps. All she'd done was recommend a doctor who specialized in internal medicine, and scheduled Cassidy for some tests at the local hospital -- which Cassidy promptly canceled.

She didn't need tests done on her abdomen. What she needed was a gynecologist who knew what they were talking about.

What she needed was more time.

Wedding planning with Margo had sucked up the last meager drops of her free time. The rest of her schedule was chock full with school and work. She didn't have time to be dealing with stupid cramps.

Cassidy followed her friends out of the limo, straightening the little tiara on her head as she stood. She felt a familiar pang in her stomach and a simultaneous pressure behind her eyes. *What the hell? Tonight? I am not dealing with whatever menstrual headaches my body throws at me tonight. Tonight, I am having fun.*

Margo pulled on Cassidy's hand, tugging her towards the line of eager club-goers that wrapped around the city block. Cassidy let herself be pulled along across the pavement, shivering once as a strong gust of wind blew down the block. Her black high-heeled boots clicked loud and clear in the crisp October night air, and Cassidy enjoyed the sound. It had been fun taking the fancy boots from the back of her closet, and she was satisfied with the sound they made and the inch they added to her height.

Becky led the way up to the bouncer, and explained something to him. Cassidy saw the bouncer talk into his little earpiece, and then he opened the ropes to them. Margo cinched Cassidy in to her hip, and together along with their group of girls, they followed Becky into the club.

The lights were dim, and loud music was thumping. Cassidy knew that Becky had reserved some kind of back room. Cassidy had never been to the Metro Disco before, but she saw that it was a hot venue. It was Saturday night, and the place was packed.

Becky was greeted by a man with greased back hair, a shiny blue shirt, and a clipboard. He waved them forward, and Becky in turn beckoned the girls.

Cassidy was overwhelmed by the music, the lights, and the luxurious club setting. Low mirrored tables, chic black leather furniture, and even modern low beds made her wonder what kind of a place they'd rented. She let go of Margo as they entered the back room. There was one circular booth, mirrors, a full bar, and even a personal bartender.

He reminded Cassidy of a statue as he waited for the girls to remove their jackets and find seats in the round booth. Cassidy squeezed in next to Becky.

"How in the world did you manage this place?" she asked her friend.

"It's this guy I'm seeing," answered Becky, pleasure apparent in her voice. "He owns the place, along with some other guys. He owns a bunch of clubs. Not only that... he hired some dancers for us."

Cassidy raised an eyebrow. She knew that Becky was the wildest in their group, but this was pushing the limits, even for her. "Dancers, Beck?"

The bartender had come to life and was now crushing mint in the bottom of a glass bowl. The music that was playing for them swirled through the air, feeding energy into the luxurious setting. Cassidy felt like she was a movie star.

Mojitos were passed around and Cassidy didn't dare take a sip. Alcohol triggered the headaches she'd been dealing with, and she wanted to last the whole night. This was a big memory for her friend. Soon they'd all be on a plane to the Dominican, and then Margo would be a wife.

She had to treasure this last night on the town with her Margo.

Many photos, speeches, dancing, and several mojitos later, the lights dimmed further and the music shifted to a sexy, slow, rhythmic beat. Suddenly the doors open. Six men walked in to the beat of the music, and began dancing for them. Margo put her hands up in the air, apparently feeling the music, the drinks, and the thrill of being the bachelorette. Cassidy laughed, watching her friend's faces as the men removed first their shirts, and then their pants. They were now just in black, barely there g-strings.

They're good strippers, Cassidy thought, though she'd never seen dancers like this before and had nothing to compare to.

Becky was holding up money, and one of the ripped, waxed, tanned men came close to her, giving Becky full view of all of his goods. Cassidy was glad that she had a place deep in the booth, and could remain a mere observer of the action.

When the private show was over, the girls were ready to join the massive crowd that was now enjoying the music and lights of the Metro. Cassidy was happy to be out into the wider arena. She was determined to enjoy the night with her friend, but the music was becoming a little too much for her head. She felt a headache coming on. She went to the bar, and ordered a Perrier with lime, thinking that maybe getting some hydration would help her to fight it off.

It wasn't until she'd received the drink and then turned to survey the scene that she noticed the handsome stranger across the bar. He was tall, blonde, and extremely handsome, in a rebellious, off-kilter kind of way. He didn't seem to be enjoying the music; he was alert, as if meant business. She watched him for several minutes. He was surveying the crowd in sweeping motions, intently. He was an observer, like herself.

She was intrigued.

He seemed to notice her watching, and met her eyes. Embarrassed that she'd been caught staring, she looked down to her drink.

When she looked up, he was gone.

THREE

Zeb watched the girl in the pink-jeweled tiara, smiling to himself as he saw her look to the place he had been sitting. He was making his way to her. How could he not? It had been hours, and the club showed no signs of slowing. He'd much rather spend his time waiting talking to a pretty girl.

She was more than pretty. She seemed to be glowing, with some kind of an aura that pulled him towards her.

He could see her body, now that he was rounding the bar and approaching her. She was curvaceously plump, and everything about her looked like it would be soft to the touch. Her pale skin looked smooth as porcelain, and her dark, waved hair was silky as it poured over her shoulders. She wore tight jeans and a sparkling black top. As he walked up to her, and she lifted her eyes to meet his again, he saw they were dark, and lined with coal-black eyeliner which was lifted up at the sides, catlike.

She was stunning.

Without a word he found a place next to her. She'd looked back to her drink, and was stirring it nervously with the straw.

The music was too loud, and he leaned close, wanting to introduce himself. As he leaned in he saw her grimace. She put a beautifully manicured hand to her temple.

She looked hurt.

16

"Are you alright?" he asked, as he leaned close instead of properly introducing himself. She looked like she was experiencing intense pain.

"Yeah," she whispered as she sucked air in through her teeth and grabbed her head again. "I get these headaches once in a while. I think it's this music." She took a few deep breaths.

"Are they migraines?" Zeb asked. He had a lot of experience, as a neurosurgeon, in dealing with headaches. "If you try some aspirin and a glass of soda, the caffeine might actually help."

"Thanks. I'll just... I think I really need some air."

"Follow me," Zeb said, forgetting his Darrious-tracking mission for a moment and leading her towards the back exit.

He pushed the large metal door open and felt cool air greet them. Relief, even for him, was instant. It was wonderful to get away from the crowd, the loud music, and even the hot charged air of the club.

The tiara girl seemed to feel it too. She let out a sigh and leaned against the cool cement building. He found a place next to her, watching her face carefully for more signs of pain.

After a few more deep breaths, she spoke. "I think it might pass. Shit." She looked frustrated. "I should be in there with Margo. I'm so lame."

"You're not lame." *You're gorgeous*, he wanted to say, but held back.

"Ouch!" she exclaimed.

Zeb could tell from her face that the pain had returned, and that it was serious. "Do you want me to call someone for you? Is there someone inside who could take you home, or to the hospital?"

"I don't need the hospital. I've been having these for over a year, since I started my masters program. I thought it was stress at first... but now..." Her voice trailed off and she shook her head.

"Where are they located? What do they feel like?"

"Kind of around my eyes. That's why I thought it was school... all the reading you know. They're just getting worse lately, and there are these weird flashes of light. It's a pain in the ass, really, but not hospital-worthy. I just have to get through my friend's wedding and then I'll make an appointment or something."

"Are you in the wedding party?"

She eyed him warily, and he could tell that she was suspicious of his interest. He remembered that to her, he was a stranger at a club. He'd gone into doctor-mode, as if he was in the hospital interviewing a patient who would reveal every single detail of their lives gladly. But she didn't know that he was a doctor. He backtracked.

"Not that it's any of my business. I... sorry I'll let you be. If you need anything, I'm right over here. I think I need some air too."

He left it at that, and gave her some space. He walked away and pretended to check his phone so that he looked busy.

Soon she came up to him, still holding her head. "You know that soda you offered? Can you go try to grab one? This isn't getting any better and I hate to bother one of the girls."

Zeb was happy to feel useful. He walked in and ordered the soda, checking for Darrious as he waited. He located him after just a moment, chatting up a table of guests.

When he returned to the tiara girl and handed her the glass, she took it gratefully.

"It just takes a few minutes because the caffeine has to be processed by your stomach lining before it can enter your bloodstream and make it into your brain. You should feel some relief in ten to fifteen minutes, max," said Zeb.

"Wow, you sound like an actual doctor," she laughed. He just laughed along with her. *No need to get into that now*, he thought.

Instead of leaving again as she sipped the soda, he decided to stay at her side. She seemed to be warming up to him. "What do you do?"he asked, "for work?"

"I'm a student, mostly," she said, motioning up the road. "At McGill. But when I'm not at studying I work at a sweets shop down on Main Street. La Belle Vie. Do you know it?"

Zeb shook his head.

She continued, "Oh, you're really missing out. It's fancy chocolates -- really good ones, with cream filling, caramel, and nuts... if you like nuts. But they're very careful in the kitchen, so as not to mix. You know, for those customers with allergies. I'm rambling, aren't I?" she seemed flustered and blushed, waving her hand in front of her face.

"What field are you studying?" Zeb asked. He wanted her to keep talking. He loved her sweet voice. A sweet shop would suit her perfectly. She could imagine her behind the counter. If he lived in this city, he'd visit regularly just to hear her talk about the fillings.

"Psychology," she answered him. "I'm getting my masters in child psychology."

Wow, thought Zeb. *Not only is she drop-dead gorgeous, but she's kind and smart too.* He was impressed by the way she acted towards him. He'd had trouble with women who seemed interested in him just because he was a doctor. But as relationships progressed it always turned out that they were more interested in his paycheck and prestige than the man behind the mask. He liked the way the girl was talking to him, even without knowing his profession.

She tilted her head back to look up at the sky, and let out a long sigh. "I think it's passing," she said, a look of obvious relief crossing over her face.

"I'm glad," he said. He meant it.

He barely knew her, but he hated to see her in pain.

"That really helped. Thank you. I owe you." She looked deeply into his eyes for the first time, and Zeb couldn't help but look directly back to her. He felt lost for a moment, and forgot where he was, what he was doing, and why he was sitting on a curb outside of a club in Montreal.

All he knew was that she was looking into him, and he could feel a sense of connection with her stirring somewhere deep inside of him.

He felt like the girl in the tiara was looking deep into his soul.

He felt like time stopped for a moment. When it passed, he shook his head, forcing a sense of time and place to come back into his mind.

Did she feel that too? he wondered. Afraid he'd been acting strangely, he stood. "Can I help you up?"

She shook her head. "I don't think I'm ready for that music again. It's kind of nice out here."

He was going to walk away when she looked at him and asked, "Would you mind keeping me company?"

He didn't say it out loud, but that was exactly what he wanted to do. He was tired of waiting inside the club for Darrious. Besides, as they'd been talking he had noticed that the navy blue Porsche Darrious drove was parked along the curb a ways down the alley. Zeb recognized it from previous visits. Extortionist visits.

He'd been watching carefully in the club, surveying Darrious' every move. But now he was watching the girl in the tiara. He didn't want it to distract him from his mission, but he did want to hear her sweet voice more, and see that smile. The club was hours from shutting down, and Darrious had been managing the crowds, bouncing between the various private rooms, the bar, the DJ, and the back office, with no signs of slowing. As a business man, he seemed to be thorough about his job; Zeb had to hand him that. He could watch the Porsche instead of Darrious himself, he justified. And that way, he could stay right next to her.

Looking down at the woman next to him, he was swept away with desire to feel her soft, plump lips. They were so kissable, and she was so present, there with him. He felt lucky to be passing the time with her.

"What do you do?" she asked.

He hesitated, and realized that he didn't want to tell her that he was a doctor. He was enjoying the way she treated him without knowing. So he told her something else about himself, instead.

"Well, that's kind of why I am here," he said, surprised at his own honesty. But what did he have to lose? She lived in another country, and in all likelihood he would never see her again. Yes, he was attracted to her, but a relationship was not in the cards for him. She was listening with apparent curiosity.

He took breath, and kept going. "I used to work for the guy who owns this club, Darrious. It's the way I paid for college, and then even for -- " he was about to say 'med school' but caught himself, "other things. My mom isn't well, and she needs a lot of full time care -- her health and what-not." He brushed this aside, not wanting to go into his mother's saga, for his own emotional sake. "So I found that working for Darrious I could make a lot of cash. And fast. I mean, if I worked parties, I could make a few grand in a weekend. Which meant I could study, and pay for my mom's care, and..."

"Parties?" she asked hesitantly.

"I was a stripper," he confessed, almost laughing out loud of the absurdity of it. The look of shock on her face was obvious, and this caused him to feel embarrassment. *This is why I don't want anyone to know!* he thought, chiding himself for confessing so openly to someone he barely knew. Something about her made him want to talk forever. She was a good listener, but even so he could see that he had told her more than he should have.

She was staring incredulously. "You mean you -- really?"

Just then the door slammed open, and Darrious spilled into the alley way.

He was dragging a man behind him, by the shirt collar. He threw him onto the pavement as the door closed with a bang behind them.

Before Darrious turned and could see them, Zeb jumped to his feet. He pulled the girl up, into the shadows with him, and held her there. He noticed her flinch as he held her around the waist, and he lessened his grip. He held her, watching Darrious deliver a firm kick into the man's stomach. The man skittered back, away from Darrious, and then stood.

"Don't come back to dees estableeshment!" Darrious spat in English with a thick French accent.

A woman exited the club a moment later, as Darrious was watching the man run down the street. She latched onto Darrious's arm. Zeb heard murmuring and protest from Darrious as the woman lead him away. She kissed his neck and then wove her hands through his hair as she kissed him hungrily on the lips.

Darrious gave into her pleas and let himself be lead away from the club. Still kissing, they fumbled their way towards the navy Porsche.

Zeb could not waste a moment. This is what he was here for. He had to get pictures. Nothing that Darrious could refute. He had to get a shot of the woman in Darrious's bed.

The past is the past. I have a new life now, Zeb thought resolutely. He took tiara girl's hand and lead her back to the metal doors.

Without thinking, he cupped her face in his hands. "I hope that you feel better soon," he said, looking deeply into her eyes. The feel of her face in his hands was wonderful. He wanted to say more, to thank her for keeping him company, and for listening to him, but changed his mind.

"Good bye," he said, looking again into her eyes before removing his hands and opening the door for her. "I don't think you should stay out here alone. Is that okay?"

She nodded.

He watched her walk through the door. He closed his eyes for a moment.

He wanted to remember her deep eyes and her sweet lips. He opened his eyes and took her all in one last time before turning and running down the street.

FOUR

He turned and ran down the street towards his motorcycle. He could see the Porsche light's turning down the street. If he hurried, he'd catch up before they got off the boulevard. *If he hurried.*

His mind was racing about the girl. Something in his subconscious was tickling its way forward, and he tried to listen to the nudges as he sped into the night in pursuit of the Porsche. He brought the thoughts forward, as he'd learned to do over the years. Her headaches, the way she'd flinched when he touched her kidneys. The flashes of light.

As always his brain was going a mile a minute with the information, and was as if on its own will, searching for the correct diagnosis.

He was eliminating possibilities as he drove, weaving in and out of traffic to catch up with the Porsche which he could see ahead. His ticket to freedom.

She'll be okay, he told himself repeatedly, but his mind kept stubbornly circling back to the problem as if the thoughts were playing on a broken record: *Tiara girl. Brain aneurism. Tiara girl. Brain aneurism.*

You're fault if she dies.
Your fault for not warning her.
Tiara girl.

In the midst of these thoughts, he simultaneously formed a plan of action on the Darrious front. Zeb hadn't graduated college at eighteen and put himself through med school because he was slow. He'd been gifted his whole life. Whether it was performing surgery in OR or problem solving a 'Darrious Situation' as he'd titled it, didn't matter. He could figure it out.

Anything.

And he didn't give up.

Cassidy was reeling.

He'd held her in his arms so tenderly. But then he'd left! Tearing after Becky and her new beau as if his life depended on it! What had it been about? Why had he followed Becky and her new boyfriend? Becky's new boyfriend did not seem like the nicest of men, to say the least.

Cassidy stood still inside the dark hallway, letting herself think about the way she'd felt when he held her. It was a delicious feeling of safety and security, and she let it wash over her for a moment. It was a feeling as if in his arms, she could be safe forever. She didn't know what do about Evan, but she knew that the way she felt in this stranger's embrace was far safer than she'd ever felt in her boyfriend's.

Usually, she felt like she was the one taking care of Evan, and not the other way around. He just always seemed to be getting into trouble, and his drama usually sucked her right along with it. After Margo's wedding, she'd talk to him.

After the wedding...

She'd been putting so much off until after the wedding.

She thought about Becky's new guy. He was violent. He had kicked a man hard in the stomach. And Becky had left with him, in that navy Porsche. *What has Beck gotten herself into this time? And why am I always the responsible one*? she wondered, taking out her phone. She had to text Beck, to ask her where she was and to tell her to be careful.

Beck? I saw your new beau taking care of some business and he doesn't seem too nice. Are you okay? Text me when you arrive at his house. I need an address.

She pressed send.

She knew that Becky was excited to finally be seeing her new man's house. Becky had mentioned that she thought he might be loaded, and Cassidy knew that she was excited to see just what his living situation was. Becky kept saying how modest he was, how he never talked about his home, and how she'd never seen it. Now Cassidy suspected that there was a different reason for the new beau's clandestine behavior. He was a first class sleaze ball. No, he didn't seem like a stand-up citizen at all.

Cassidy went back into the club, her anxiety over her friend's situation worsened by the lack of reply to the text. Her pulse was still racing from the stranger's arms. She waited nervously, checking her phone every few minutes. Nothing came through.

After a while, she looked for Margo, and found that she'd been joined by Marcus and Evan. Margo and Marcus were dancing, a happy bachelor and bachelorette, soon to be married. She loved to watch them look at each other like they were the only two people in existence. She and Evan never seemed to look at each other like that.

"Cass, Babe!" Evan had soon spotted her. "Marcus is getting shitty."

He laughed but she refused to laugh along.

"What's wrong?" Marcus asked, deadpan, as if he was annoyed that she wasn't laughing.

Did he even notice that she'd been gone? Or was he so wrapped up in the party that it had escaped his interest?

He pulled her in for a hug but she evaded his embrace by stepping away and crossing her arms over her chest.

"Don't tell me it's a headache," he complained, wary of her fragile state. For the last three months the headaches had become a sore spot in their relationship. It was as if he didn't believe that they were real. Unlike the stranger, thought Cassidy, who seemed to take her very seriously.

"It's Becky. She just got in the car with one of the club owners -- I guess she's been seeing him for a few weeks, but he's *not* a good guy."

"Becky's a grown woman. She can take care of herself."

Cassidy shook her head. "I don't think she knows what he's like, or else she'd never be into him like this." Her phone chimed and she reached into her purse and took it out.

You are right...This was a huge mistake. Can you come get me? Sorry Cass. 134 Brossard.

Cass showed Evan the text.

"Come on," she said, pulling his arm.

"We're leaving?"

"She needs us, Evan."

Rue de Brossard was quiet, upscale, and yet felt distinctly ominous to Cassidy as she pulled her camery sedan to the side of the street near number 134. She had barely opened the car door when Becky came streaming out, yelling, crying, and wrapped in a sheet. She saw Darrious behind Becky, and... was that really him? The handsome stranger from the club was running after Becky as well.

What was this all about? Cass ran towards her friend, and heard the handsome stranger calling out.

"It's not of you... I don't want pictures of you. It's this douche-bag I'm trying to nail! You know he's married?"

"Get off my property! Merde! Vous etes un intrus! Now, I call police! Get!" Darrious was yelling furiously from his doorway.

The handsome stranger seemed to be ignoring the violent outburst of mixed French and English behind him, and was still following the distraught Becky. He called out after her, "I swear, you're better off without him!"

FIVE

Zeb stopped suddenly when he saw her.

What is she doing here? he asked himself.

He walked to her, glancing between the two girls. Darrious's mistress was tear-streaked and nearly naked, while tiara girl appeared composed and strong. He hated to be the one to ruin two girl's nights, but he knew he had to speak. If he did not, his conscious would weigh heavy on him and he knew he couldn't deal with that.

His conscious was heavy enough as it was.

He looked tiara girl right in the eye.

"You're kidneys are swollen. I felt you flinch when I held you. You have headaches that gain in intensity when you look to the left, indicating a physical abnormality in your brain. This creates the feeling of pressure behind your eyes. You're in your late twenties or early thirties. You're not drinking alcohol at a bachelorette party, so I'm guessing it exacerbates your symptoms. You have Polycystic Kidney Disease, adult onset. I am guessing you have blood in your urine. Am I correct?"

"How did you --"

"You need to have your brain checked for aneurysms. Judging by your facial expressions, your headache episodes are severe which indicates that it is large in size. You need to have it fixed as soon as possible or it may burst, which could kill you. I'm sorry to be the bearer of bad news. I could be wrong." *But I rarely ever am*, he thought.

30

He had delivered the speech on autopilot, putting up barriers against her bewilderment, her pained expression, and the way she stepped backwards as he talked. He knew that was he was saying was repulsive. This was the opposite of what he wanted to do to her, this woman who was so very attractive. But he also knew that if he did not speak, guilt would further burden him. Besides, as a doctor he'd gotten used to being the bearer of bad news.

As the three of them stood in shocked silence, the car door opened and a guy in a plaid button up shirt and short dark hair walked towards them. Tiara girl held her hand over her mouth, and was stepping away from Zeb, towards the man in plaid. The plaid shirted guy looked from the girls to Zeb, unsure of what was going on, but seeing that tiara girl was very upset.

Zeb was forming an explanation in his mind, but he didn't have much time to think before the plaid shirted guy then punched Zeb solidly in the nose.

Zeb hit the ground. Pain exploded in his head and back as he hit the cement. He saw the guy guiding tiara girl away. The man in plaid got into the passenger seat, but just before Cassidy opened the driver's door, Zeb called out, "Stop!"

Zeb pushed himself up. He needed to get the last part out.

"One more thing!" he managed to call out, pausing to wipe blood away from his mouth as it dripped form his nose. "Don't lift anything heavier than twenty pounds. That could cause it to burst. And definitely don't get on an airplane. If you do, you're risking your life."

He laid back, the message delivered, and the picture of Darrious cheating safely in his pocket. All in all, the mission had been a success. He'd gotten what he'd come for. He felt relief that he'd seen the girl again, and could now clear his mind from the thoughts about her diagnosis that had been plaguing him.

He'd said his piece, and the rest was up to her... and her boyfriend, whom apparently she had forgotten to mention in their two hour talk behind the club.

I guess we both had things that we didn't want to say, he thought, pushing himself up, off of the sidewalk.

As he walked towards the car, he saw something sparkling on the ground.

Her tiara.

He picked it up and put it in the pocket of his leather jacket. He thought about the way her soft, cherub-like face had felt cupped in his hands. He thought of the way she had looked so deeply into his soul.

Did she fail to mention her boyfriend because she was attracted to me? he wondered. *Does it matter?* He would never see her again. Maybe it was good that she had a boyfriend; at least she didn't have to handle the news alone. He tried to feel glad that at least she had some support for the battle that he knew she'd be facing in the weeks and months to come.

Six

Zeb checked the mirror once more before putting his stethoscope around his neck and pinning his badge on. The bruise on his face had gone down a little, but he still had a cut on his cheek. The guy must have been wearing a ring. The cut was right below his left eye. He touched it lightly with his index finger.

The pictures had turned out wonderfully. He'd emailed Darrious, threatening to expose the pictures if the blackmail continued. Partly, Zeb wanted to send the pictures to his wife anyways, but he thought that would be pushing his luck. He just wanted to be free from the blackmail of his old boss, not get wrapped farther into his life. He wanted nothing to do with the whole scene. He was a respectable doctor. He had his whole future ahead of him.

He felt a hand clap him on his shoulder. "You okay, buddy?" Jack asked. Jack had relaxed a lot since he started dating Danielle, the neurosurgery program's first year resident, but Zeb still wasn't quite back to calling him buddy.

As Chief Resident, Jack Pace was essentially Zeb's boss. He was the disciplinarian, the scheduler, and the person who held the power to delay his progress in the residency program. Jack was older than Zeb, but Zeb was mature for his age, at least in work terms. Like Zeb, Jack was extremely smart. Zeb appreciated Jack's intellect, and the two had been good friends before Jack became the Chief Resident.

Since Jack had become Chief, Zeb kept his guard up when it came to conversations with Jack. It wasn't the way he wanted it, but it was the way it had to be.

"Getting better. Thankful I didn't break it. That'd really look bad."

"What was it again -- an accident on the tennis court?" Jack raised his eyebrows, clearly doubting Zeb's sporting injury story.

"Something like that," Zeb mumbled. He hated to lie, but could think of no way to explain his busted-up face.

"As long as your brain is okay. We've all come to rely on your smarts around here," Jack said, as the two men entered the hallway.

"I promise, it's just cosmetic," Zeb said.

"How is the OR looking this week?" Jack asked, touching on business for a moment.

"Packed. Monday, Wednesday, and Thursday. I've got tomorrow off for teaching, and Friday is my on call day and night. You on call this weekend?" Zeb asked. He liked working his overnights with Jack.

Jack shook his head. "Danielle and I are going out of town. It's you and Sondra. Hey -- I know you're on your way to the OR now, but I have a consult that I'd love your opinion on. She'll be on your schedule by the end of the week, by the looks of the case, so you may as well meet her now. Got twenty minutes?"

Zeb checked his watch. "Sure," he said, following Jack up into the staircase to North Nine.

They kept up a good pace, and once on the neuro floor, headed straight into a patient room.

As soon as they entered, Zeb stopped in his tracks.

His eyes widened as he stared at the figure sitting up on the bed.

It was tiara girl; the girl that he had held! He felt like he could still feel the heat of her in his arms, could still smell her hair, and could see the crushed look on her face when he'd changed her life forever.

He knew the way people looked when they knew something had changed that could never be fixed. His mom had had the same expression when his dad had left them. And life had never been the same.

He knew it wouldn't be for the girl either.

When she saw him, her expression flash through a range of emotion. He saw a look of recognition sparkle in her eyes. This changed to surprise, and then a flash of anger.

Emotions from their first meeting came rushing back to him -- the way she'd looked that night, the way she smiled and laughed and opened up to him.

And here she is, right in front of me.

She took my advice.

"You," she said.

Then she picked up a water pitcher and threw it at him.

"Cassidy Novotny," Jack read aloud from her chart, as the water pitcher hit Zeb in the chest and ice water burst out all over him. "Do you know Zeb here?"

"We've met," she said, glaring at Zeb.

Zeb didn't know what to do. He looked around for a towel but not finding one, used his hands to wipe futilely at the water dripping down his coat. The plastic water pitcher clattered to a halt on the floor.

Neither Cassidy nor Zeb spoke, and Jack pressed forward. "Well, I can *see* that you two know each other."

"Yes, we've met" said Zeb. "Cassidy," he said, and held out his hand. "I don't know if I've properly introduced myself. I am Doctor Zeb Morgan and I work with Doctor Pace, Doctor Wineright, and Luthar Hart here at Baily Mills. I see you have considered my message."

"Message?" Jack asked, looking back and forth between the two.

Cassidy nodded warily. "Yes, I did. You said I might be dying, so I looked up Doctor Hart and made an appointment. 'Doctor' Morgan? You're telling me you're a real, legitimate doctor? All that time we -- "

"Yes," interrupted Zeb, before she could say anything about the club. "I am." He showed her his badge and she looked from the badge to his eyes.

"What else would he be?" asked Jack.

"Well, the last time I saw Doctor Morgan he was telling me—"

"In Montreal," Zeb interrupted again. "We met in Montreal. It's so good to see you here in Burlington. I didn't expect that you'd come to the states for medical care."

"My parents live here, and recommended Harts work."

"It is helpful to have family nearby," said Jack. "Especially if you chose to get surgery. Support is key for recovery." He was pulling up a stool near Cassidy, and Zeb was still standing across from her.

Jack sat on the stool and continued to looked back and forth between them with confusion. After a moment, when the situation did not become any clearer, he stood and motioned to Jack with a tilt of his chin towards the hallway. "Zeb, can I see you for a minute? In the hallway?" he asked.

Cassidy crossed her arms over her chest as she watched Doctor Pace lead the handsome stranger into the hallway.

She was angry with him. She resented him for presenting the truth -- a truth that she'd been working hard to deny for a long time: that something was wrong with her.

But now she had to face it, or else she could die.

Cassidy could not believe the nerve of this Doctor Morgan, who had said those awful things to her.

He had told her not get on the flight.

She had been more than tempted to ignore his warning. As she, Evan, and Becky had packed into her car on the night of the bachelorette party, Evan asked her for the story. Becky sobbed about the shock of having a man jump out with a camera. She explained that Darrious was married

Cassidy had told her friend that she had seen Darrious kick a man in the stomach, and they all decided that Becky was better off without the corrupt club owner.

It was a rough end to the night, and Cassidy had tried to push the stranger's words from her mind. She distracted herself with the drama of her friend's situation. But she couldn't keep it out of her mind for long. She tried to push his diagnosis away, and tell herself that he was just a crazy washed up stripper from a club, and that he didn't know what he was talking about.

Evan had asked her about her mood, and she was too afraid to repeat the stranger's message. She dealt with enough drama in her life, she didn't want to create her own. The guy was crazy. She didn't even know him.

But now, here he is.

A doctor!

He did not look like a doctor, and he hadn't said anything about that at the club. But he had known exactly how to make her headaches better. And yet, the way he'd held her, had talked to her, and looked at her made her feel... good. He seemed to care. The way he had connected with her was different than anything she'd ever known.

And he said do not get on an airplane.

She found herself thinking more and more about his words as the Monday morning flight departure time neared. She called her mother, to ask for advice. She had barely been able to repeat the story before breaking down into panicked sobs. Her mother hadn't been very helpful at them time, but apparently had used Sunday as a research day, and she'd called Cassidy back on Monday morning. She left a message saying that she had booked an appointment for Cassidy in Burlington, Vermont, at Baily Mills Hospital.

Cass had listened to her mother's voicemail, her hand shaking as she disconnected. She couldn't get her legs to walk into the line-up of passengers waiting to board the flight. She pulled Evan aside, and told him her decision, pressing his ticket into his hand.

"I can't go," she said. "I'm too sick right now. I'm not feeling well."

Evan had been confused, and said that they could both exchange their tickets, reschedule and join their group the next day. Or the day after. The wedding wasn't until Friday. He didn't understand.

She'd shaken her head, emphatically. "Go. Go with Marcus. You're the best man. I need to you to tell Margo that I am sorry. I will call the hotel and talk to her once you all arrive. I'm sorry, I just can't get on that plane. Go."

She didn't say why.

She didn't tell him about the aneurism.

The line of passengers was filtering past , and the wedding party was waiting, looking at them impatiently.

The airport worker called out that it was the last chance to board, and it had all been so rushed. She waved them forward and Margo and Marcus boarded. Becky trailed along with the other members of the party. Cass had watched her friends enter the plane, and had watched Evan reluctantly join them.

"I'll call you when we get there. We'll change your ticket. You'll be feeling better soon," he called out. Then he ran back and kissed her, quickly on the lips. She pushed him forward and he ran to get through the line before the stewardess blocked the way.

She had called her mother, next, and drove to her parents house in Burlington. Her parents had rushed her to the appointment. Now here she was, just a few hours after her flight departure time.

Pissed that she was missing it all.

Pissed that she had taken a chance and believed him when he said that she shouldn't fly, that she should get checked out.

Most of all, terrified that his diagnosis was right.

Tell a girl she might be dying, and then leave? she thought furiously. *Who does that?* But she remembered that Evan had punched him. He'd been flat out on the sidewalk, and she had been the one to leave first. Things had been so mixed up, so confusing. She hadn't even known his name, that night. All she'd known about him was that he used to be a stripper.

And now here he was, a real doctor!

This was frightening because it meant that he might really know what he was talking about.

Zeb followed Jack out of the room into the hallway.

"Something you need to tell me, Zeb?" Jack asked.

Zeb hesitated. He and Jack used to be so close. They'd survived the first few years of neurosurgery residency be relying heavily on each other, and Jack had been his closest friend. But lately, Jack was all business. He took the role of Chief Resident seriously, and seemed to be removing himself from the role of friend.

Zeb saw Jack read his face, and knew that his quick friend was figuring out the guard that Zeb put up between them.

"Let me ask you this," Jack tried again. "You don't have to tell me anything that you don't want to, about whatever connection you have with Cassidy Novotny. But you do have to tell me if you feel in good consciousness that there is any reason why you should *not* be on her care team. Is there a reason that you should *not* continue with this case?"

Zeb thought about it. He and Cassidy barely knew each other. He'd have to hope that she would not mention his past as a stripper. He thought of how he'd held her face; of how much he'd wanted to kiss her. But had they really crossed any lines? No. Long eye gazes or attraction was nothing concrete. He could be imagining all of it – and plus, she had a boyfriend.

I'm in the clear, thought Zeb. *Aren't I?*

"I'm good to go, Pace. I've seen her once, in a social setting, but nothing happened between us that would cause this to be an issue," he told his superior.

Jack raised an eyebrow. "You're sure about that? She seemed to be pretty fired up about something."

"I'm sure we'd be fired up too, if we found out we had a kidney condition as well as a near to exploding blood vessel in our brains that might kill us at any moment," Zeb stated.

"True," said Jack.

Zeb saw Jack process this. Zeb never was one to sugar-coat things. They dealt with life and death, so why not be blunt about it? He liked to say things as they were.

Jack whistled under his breath, shaking his head. "Was that your message to her... at this social setting?"

"I noticed the symptoms. I put two and two together. I told her I might be wrong."

"I guess that's what we have to figure out," said Jack, turning to head back into the room. "Let's get this assessment done. I know you need to get to the OR, and we have to put an order in for contrast from pharmacy. Wineright wants her prepped for angio by three pm."

Zeb waited for Jack to turn and step back into the room. He needed a moment alone, to gather himself.

He raked his hand through his hair, taking a deep breath. *Let this go well*, he silently requested. *What have I gotten myself into?*

He stood a little straighter and walked back into the room, noticing that when Cassidy wasn't throwing things at him or glaring, she looked very sweet and innocent. She had less makeup on, and although he'd loved her smoky eyes at the club, they looked beautiful naturally as well.

He was surprised at how relieved he was to see her. Though he'd tried to ignore it, he realized that he had been worried about her.

41

He helped Jack complete the exam, and held the chart, writing notes while Jack checked her reflexes, pupils, and continued asking questions.

"Diminished reflexes, left side" Jack reported, shining the light into Cassidy's eyes.

"Is that bad?" Cassidy whispered, and Zeb hated hearing the fear in her voice. She seemed to have slightly gotten over the surprise of seeing him.

But not entirely.

She kept on stealing glances at him. He saw her looking when he wrapped the blood pressure cuff around her arm. He felt a charge run through him when his fingers brushed her skin as he secured the cuff. He felt the memory whisper between them, of holding her close in the alleyway. He remembered the way it seemed that it was only them. He remembered how right her body had felt tucked in warmly next to his.

Jack excused himself and this left just Zeb and Cassidy in the room.

"You're blood pressure is normal. When was your last headache?" asked Zeb.

"Two nights ago," Cassidy answered. "After you said... we drove home, and... well I had one later that night."

"What were you doing at the time?" Zeb continued.

"I was researching... kidney disease and headaches, just like you said. I was... I was crying."

"I'm sorry," Zeb said, his heart breaking. She seemed upset just remembering it. It must have been horrible, scary, and nerve wracking to receive news like he'd delivered.

"I didn't know how else to tell you. I didn't know if I would ever see you again. I had to let you know."

"Like that?"

"What else could I have done?"

She seemed to think, and came up with nothing. Her anger dissipated as she saw his point. It had been a brutally direct message, but it hadn't quite been the time or place for a more professional one.

"I'm glad you warned my about the plane. If this is true, and I have a --" she hesitated, as if it was difficult to keep speaking. After a moment she pressed on. "If I have an... aneurism, it's good that I know, because I was about to get on a plane this morning –- to the Dominican Republic, for my friend's wedding."

Thank God I said something, Zeb thought to himself. "I'm sorry you'll be missing the wedding. And again, I'm really sorry for telling you like that. I know it must have been a hard thing to process, so out of the blue like that. You must have been scared."

"It's okay." She wiped a tear away. "My... my boyfriend was there."

She couldn't put it off any longer. She could sense by the way he was looking at her that he was still interested. The way he'd been at the club, the way he'd talked to her and held her face, like he wanted to kiss her.

She should have stopped it all earlier. She had to tell him about Evan, although part of her didn't want to.

"Good," he said. "I'm glad you weren't alone. I thought about that when I was saying it; I knew it would be difficult to hear. I guess he's the guy who punched me? How long have you...? Sorry, that's none of my -- " he was floundering suddenly, the memory of the night they met had clouded his interview, and he now remembered where he was and what his role was. He cleared his throat, and restarted."I just... I thought it was better to give you the diagnosis."

"Yes. I guess so. What does it mean?"

"We'll have more information as the exam goes on and once Hart see's you. He really is known in his field for his breakthrough procedures, your parents were correct. I'm glad your parents recommended him."

And I'm glad to see you again, he thought.

She seemed to read his mind.

"Since college," she said, playing with the hem of her blanket. "My boyfriend Evan and I... we've been seeing each other since college."

"That's a long time. Three or four years?"

"Five," she sighed. He could read from the sigh that this was not a welcome fact. She lay back in the bed. "I'm kind of glad that I'm not there with all of them. We've been friends since college. Since we all stayed in Montreal instead of returning to our hometowns, we all just kind of gravitated together. Especially when Marcus and Margo got so serious."

Zeb loved the sound of her voice, but none the less he couldn't't' help glance at his watch.

"I'm rambling," she said, a blush creeping into her cheeks. "You don't need to hear my whole life story."

"I have to get to the OR," he said.

"I am glad you're my doctor. I almost have trouble believing it. You look so young."

"I hear that a lot." Zeb said. "I'm twenty nine. I graduated high school and college early."

"I just thought... you know you said you used to be a stripper, and I --"

"My colleagues don't exactly know that about me, so if you don't mind--"

"It's between us," she assured him. "I didn't know you lived in Burlington either. We didn't really talk about that much that night, did we? Even though we talked for two hours."

"It was the best two hours I've had in a while," he said, the words slipping out before he could censor them. *She has a boyfriend; not to mention she's your patient you dumbass,* he scolded himself internally.

To his surprise, she actually smiled. "Me too," she said.

SEVEN

After Doctor Morgan left the room, Cassidy felt like she'd had the wind knocked out of her lungs. Her handsome stranger... was an actual doctor. *Her* doctor! It didn't make sense. Nothing made sense -- he way she was sitting in Vermont, far from her apartment, her friends, classes, the chocolate shop, and Evan -- everything was spun up on its head.

She was afraid.

Ever since seeing he'd said those things to her, Saturday night, she'd been losing her mind. Everything seemed to slow down and speed up at the same time. She wasn't sure if this was real. It seemed like a dream.

The thought of Evan made her feel heavy. Why hadn't she confided in him? Why hadn't she looked to him for support with the confusion that she was going through? He would call soon, from the Dominican, and she would have to tell him the truth.

What truth?

That she was getting a diagnostic work-up. That was all she knew right now, so that was all she would say.

The truth was, she didn't want him to rush home. He'd be home soon enough. The wedding was Friday night, and they'd all return on Saturday. Except for Margo and Marcus of course; they'd be honeymooning. But Evan would be home -- in just six days -- and she wasn't ready for that. She realized that she needed the space from him. She needed to re-evaluate where they were and where they were going.

They were friends, it was true, and their social circle fit well with work, with school, with where she lived. It had all fallen so naturally and seamlessly into place.

But something was missing.

When she was constantly rushing from class to the chocolate shop, home and to the bar, there was no time to dwell on the void, but in still moments she noticed the creeping awareness that Evan was not what she was looking for. She realized that somewhere deep down, she knew that more was possible. With Evan there was no deep connection.

Not like... not like the connection that she could feel with the handsome stranger; her doctor. What was his name again? She'd come to think of him simply as *the handsome stranger*.

Doctor Morgan.

Zeb, that was it.

Even just his name sent shivers up and down her spine. The way he looked at her just drove her crazy. There was something there with him, she just could not put her finger on what it was.

He seemed to care about her -- more than a doctor should.

She liked the way he looked in his white coat. He had blonde hair, spiked up on the end, and a mischievous, daring look about him, even dressed professionally instead of in leather as he'd been when she met him. He was slightly rebellious in his style and body language, and that look couldn't be tamed by a mere white coat and shiny badge. She'd noticed some tension between he and the other doctor.

He had icy blue eyes that seemed to have the depth, like staring into an arctic sea. She wondered what was hidden inside of him. She wondered, in a fleeting fantasy, what he was like in bed. She could imagine that beneath his clothes he was quite muscular. She had felt that when he had held her, in the alley behind the club.

She thought again of how he'd held her face, and imagined kissing him.

She imagined being lost in his kiss, how all-encompassing his embrace would be, how full of life and energy he would be. She started to day dream about what his body would look like and feel like, naked

She became lost in these thoughts of Doctor Morgan, and let herself daydream.

In the afternoon, as people went in and out of the room, getting her prepped for her MRA, her mother joined her, and her father soon after. Cassidy was glad for their presence, as doctors and nurses rattled off foreign sounding terms and asked her to sign paper after paper.

There was no sign of Doctor Morgan.

As Cassidy was wheeled down the hall into procedure waiting room, she said a silent prayer that she would see *him* again. No one made her feel more safe than Zeb Morgan.

Zeb pulled the schedule off of the wall and checked to see where he was needed next.

'Novotny, Magnetic Resonance Angiography' he read.

Luis, the anesthetist peered over his shoulder. The two had worked together for years. Luis snapped his gum, an annoying habit that Zeb had learned to deal with.

"Wineright's consult. Girl in her twenties with a possible aneurysm," Luis explained as he read over Zeb's shoulder.

48

Oh, I'm aware, thought Zeb, looking up from the chart and scanning the room.

He knew, without looking, that she wasn't there yet. He'd realized that he could feel her presence. When she was around him, the air took on a different quality -- charged and pleasant, and he could feel her eyes on him. He didn't feel that now, and so knew that she wasn't there.

It wasn't long before an orderly wheeled her into the waiting room.

She took his breath away yet again, and he realized that he would have to ignore his visceral reaction to her if he was going to navigate performing the angiography.

He walked towards her, as nurses helped her up onto a waiting stretcher.

"Cassidy." He began by saying her name, more for show to the nurses. He could tell from her face that they were on a different level, a different page than the rest of the people around them. It was like a private world. "How are you feeling?" he asked, a hand on her bed rail.

"I'm okay. Hungry, I guess. I haven't been able to eat today."

"You'll be able to eat after you're done with the test. Has the procedure been explained to you?"

"Yes, I think so..."

"We're going to put you under conscious sedation. Luis here --"

At this Luis reached his hand forward, and Cassidy shook it cautiously.

"--Is going to administer a mixture of medazolam and fentanyll. This means that you will be able to respond to commands, but won't feel pain, and will not remember the procedure once it is done. I will insert a catheter, which is a very small thin plastic tube, in through one of

49

your arteries and up through your aorta, into the veins that supply oxygen to the brain. We will use pressure to inject contrast in through the catheter so that we can take pictures of the blood flow in your brain, which will show us any abnormalities."

"Like an aneurysm. You already told me I had one."

"And I said I could be wrong," said Zeb. "This will confirm it either way. Like I said, you won't feel pain, but you might be stiff or sore after the procedure because you will be lying still. You might also notice warmth in your veins, as the contrast clears out of your system. We'll deliver a local anesthetic to your groin area as well so that the initial puncture won't hurt. You might feel a pinch from the needle. Does this all sound okay to you?"

She nodded, and he wondered if she was nervous at the thought of himself doing something around her -- female parts. This seemed too personal, but he reminded himself that he was her doctor and nothing more. She was his patient. No need to make such a fuss out of it.

He reviewed the risks of the procedure as they wheeled her towards the procedure room, although they'd already been read over in the room when Cassidy had signed the consent forms.

Cassidy felt nervous when his hands reached for the blanket, and gently pulled it up and to the side. The tinge of butterflies in her stomach and nerves as he exposed her skin was a nice relief from the heavy worry she felt due to the looming test. Not only was she not looking forward to the dye being pushed through her veins, she was dreading the results.

Would the tests confirm her worst fear?

Or was he wrong?

Please, let him be wrong.
Let this all be a silly mistake.

He was respectful of her privacy. A curtain had been pulled, and a nurse helped by asking Cassidy to remove her underwear and place it in a bag. She was glad she'd shaved and also glad in some weird way that she'd worn nice, simple, black bikini briefs; they weren't too showy, or embarrassing. She carefully removed them, and the nurse put a blue papery cloth over Cassidy's groin area. Doctor Morgan taped the drape in place, and finally just the section between her thigh and the line where her underwear would go was exposed.

She focused on the touch of his hand, in gloves, on her upper thigh. He was swabbing the area with something cool, and the sponge that he used felt slightly rough.

Her legs are just right, Zeb thought, unable to keep his mind from wandering.

What would it be like to be in bed with her?

What would it be like to expose more of her skin... her whole body?

Is it all so delightfully soft, full, and touchable? Is every inch of her perfect?

He had to reel himself in before his fantasy took over.

An hour later, with the MRA film in his hand, Zeb found the neurosurgery team.

The angiogram had gone smoothly. The results were just as he had suspected: Cassidy Novotny had a large aneurism right above the base of her skull.

He was thankful that she hadn't gone on the plane; the ride might have killed her. He realized that he couldn't think about that -- it hurt too much. He was getting very attached to her, beyond what good patient care required of him. His thoughts turned more and more towards a personal level when he was with her.

The team discussed the results and then started on North Nine rounds. Cassidy's room was one of the last in the hallway, and they entered late that evening.

Doctor Luthar Hart discussed options with Cassidy and her mother, while Zeb stood behind him, analyzing Cassidy's pretty face as she took in the news. Her mother was perched nervously in a plastic blue recliner. Her father had left to pick up take out for dinner.

He saw Cassidy's look of horror when Doctor Hart described the symptoms and risks of having the aneurism rupture. He explained that after the surgery, once the immediate risk was mitigated, they would have to do further tests on her kidneys. Hart spoke about adult onset polycystic kidney disease, and the options she could take in moving forward with the diagnosis.

Zeb knew how terrifying the news must be to Cassidy.

It was difficult for him to be in the room with her, but he hoped that his presence helped her in some way.

The surgery was scheduled for Saturday. This was the first opening on Hart's schedule, even considering that it was an urgent surgery. They'd pushed it forward as much as possible, and still this was the best they could do. Hart was a very in demand surgeon. Hart pointed out, however, that this delay gave Cassidy time in the hospital for further testing to be done on her kidneys, so that the team could check for any other complications that might be present due to her PKD.

Cassidy and her mother talked and agreed that it was the best course of action. Cassidy would stay in the hospital as she waited for Saturday to come.

EIGHT

Zeb was off campus on Tuesday, and did not see Cassidy, though he thought about her through the day. On Wednesday evening, after a busy day of surgeries, he was crossing the lobby, about to leave for the evening when he saw her peering into the various windows of the gift shop.

He was glad to see her.

He watched her for a moment before approaching.

She noticed him, and met his eyes. When she looked into his eyes, he was struck with the feeling that he had missed her, over the past two days.

"Do you know where I could find some chocolate?" Cassidy asked. She had been unhooked from her IV lines. She wore a loose fitting bright pink sweatshirt over her gown, and had put on soft fleecy pajama pants as well. Her hair was a mess, and her eyes were slightly puffy and red as if she'd been crying.

He realized that she needed much more than chocolate -- she needed someone to talk to. She needed a break from the barrage of testing they'd been putting her through. He greeted her and led her into the gift shop.

"It's probably not as good as your shop in Montreal," he said as they found the candy aisle."I think it's just generic mass produced... no wait, they've got some of the good stuff." He squatted down, reaching to a low corner display. "Champlain chocolates." The box was white with embossed silver mountains. He felt happy showing it to her. It was a touch of luxury in a place that was very institutional. She looked like she could use some luxury.

"Wait here," he said, standing with the box in his hands.

She'd been so lush when he'd met her, so sparkly and soft, the eyes dark and her shirt shimmering. He wished he could give her that life back, her power, and make this scary event a little less scary. He brought the chocolates to the front of the shop. There was a stand of flowers by the register, and he chose a bouquet of six cream colored carnations. He made his purchases, and returned to her with the flowers behind his back.

First he handed her the chocolates.

She looked relieved, and smiled at the ornate box.

"Oh thank goodness," she breathed out, hugging the box to her chest. "I really am having a fix. Chocolate seems to make everything better."

He wanted to kiss her, then and there, for the way she was smiling despite her circumstances. He brought the flowers forward and was pleased to see the smile grow.

"Do you want to see a special place?"he asked, as he watched her nose in a fluffy carnation.

She nodded.

"It's out this way." He led her out of the gift shop, through the lobby, and out the front doors.

The night air was warmer than he had expected. Certainly warmer than it had been that weekend in Montreal. The sun had set, and stars were peeking out of a clear, velvet black sky. A lamp post illuminated his favorite bench, on one edge of the main courtyard walkway. It faced away from the hospital, out across the green lawns with criss crossing pathways. He often at lunch on it, or escaped to it for breaks when he could.

She followed him to the bench, and when they sat she opened the box of chocolates.

"They are beautiful," she said, examining each dark square. "At La Belle Vie we sell chocolates with crushed lavender on them, and even gold."

"Gold?"

"Yes, gold leaf, little flakes of it." She was smiling at the thought. Her cherub like cheeks were lit with the soft lamp-light. He could see that she got pleasure from the memories.

"I'm going to hope that heaven is a chocolate shop," she said, thoughtfully removing a dark chocolate square and biting into it.

His eyes were drawn to her lips, as they landed on the square and biting into it, softly, gently.

"What do you think it's like?"

"Heaven?" he asked, mesmerized still as she licked her lips, finishing the sweet candy.

"Yes."

He wanted to tell her that he didn't believe in heaven --that he thought they might all just keep living on the earth until they didn't anymore. But he knew that she was facing surgery soon, and couldn't bring himself to say it, so he played along. "I think heaven would be like walking on top of white clouds. You would sink in a little, but there would be something there, to hold you up, too. But it would be soft. And it would be sunset all of the time."

"Like when you're flying... in an airplane? You look down, and it's a layer of clouds, and it feels like the whole earth and people and problems are very, very far away."

"Just like that," smiled Zeb, sinking closer to her. He wanted to put his arm around her shoulder.

"There would be no chocolate?" she asked.

"I've never considered it." He pretended to ponder the idea. *You would be there, in my version of heaven*, he thought and then wondered about where the thought had come from.

"There should be chocolate. You would be missing out if there wasn't. Sometimes, if I have had a very bad day.... I'll have a bite of chocolate and everything just feels...better. Like sunshine making a puddle disappear; evaporate. Do you want to try?"

Zeb nodded, aware that she was dancing around the subject -- her surgery -- distracting herself with sweetness and nonsense. But he wanted to help her relax there, in fantasy, for a little while. She needed it, he was sure. He didn't want to drag her back into the reality that they were in.

It was easier to forget about the surgery. He didn't want to think about it either. He wanted to pretend that all that existed in the world was this bench -- this evening -- with Cassidy next to him.

She was picking a square intently, and then held it up towards him. He opened his mouth and she held it forward, her eyes on his. He leaned in and bit into the sweetness. As he bit through the milk chocolate coating, his teeth met soft caramel, and he felt buttery sweetness spread over his taste buds.

When he pulled the bite away, a string lingered with the chocolate, and Cassidy swept it up with her finger. Her finger met his lips, and he brought his hand to hers and held it to his mouth, giving it a soft kiss.

She pulled it away, not fast, but deliberately, and he saw that he had crossed a line. Kicking himself, he vowed to keep his feelings in check. The flowers, the chocolates... he was being too forward.

She was his patient.

She might die.

He couldn't do this to himself.

He had enough to worry about.

They sat in silence, the mood changed.

She spoke again. "I'm scared, about the surgery. But you know what? I've also got some new clarity, about things." She was looking out across the green lawn. "Like work -- I always thought... I always thought that I'd stay in Canada. I moved there for college and now I've been there for so long it seemed like the logical next step. Evan is Canadian... But being back in the states is nice. Maybe I could work here. My parents would love it."

"You're parents are very nice," he said, glad for the change in the subject.

"Are your parents here? In Vermont?" she asked.

Zeb hesitated. His parents were not his favorite topic of conversation. He nodded."My mom is. She lives in assisted care. My dad is... not around."

"Why is she in assisted care?"

"She's got end stage dementia. I'm going to visit her now, actually. We don't get along that well, but at least I try to see her for dinner once a week. Probably just to make myself feel a little less guilty."

"Why does she make you feel guilty?"

"I don't know. Once my dad left, she was really depressed. I always felt like it was my fault... " He remembered that Cassidy was studying child psychology, and laughed "you are going to make a good psychologist," he said. "I just want to talk to you forever."

She smiled up at him. It seemed that she was enjoying the conversation as much as he was.

"Dementia is a hard disease to cope with, I've heard. Is that what got you interested in studying the brain?"

Zeb shook his head. "I don't know. I think there are a lot of mysteries about how the mind works. I can't say it was on a conscious level, but subconsciously, who knows?" he shrugged. "There is something that I've noticed about my mom, though : as the disease takes away her brain functioning, she's still my mom.".

"I'm sorry, Zeb." Cassidy placed a hand on his.

It felt so good to hold her hand. He let his fingers explore her hands, as he continued to talk. "That's something I wonder about when I do each surgery. No one lives in a brain. It makes me where a person lives. In memories? In the heart? Somewhere way beyond that?"

He was lost in this thought for a moment, and felt the black cloud that was his concern over his mother's condition descending over him.

He removed his hand from hers, and tucked it in his leather jacket.

"Here," she said, holding out another chocolate. "I know it doesn't *cure* anything, but it makes you feel better."

Better about my mom being like a child that I have to take care of? Zeb thought.

Better about being on my own, since I was sixteen years old?

Better about... the list could go on and on.

He doubted that the chocolate could fix the things he'd seen and done, or the anger and guilt he felt. But Cassidy's presence next to him did make him feel slightly more grounded, more real, and like a better person. She trusted him.

She held the chocolate towards him, and again he ate it out of her fingers. The flavors did ease the tension in his shoulders; the sweetness made him feel better. It was like she said – he felt a sunlight penetrate his dark mood. He knew that it was her light, not the chocolate's.

"Now you," he said. He carefully took the box from her and analyzed each square. He didn't know if she liked nuts, so he strayed from the ones with obvious bumps. He chose a smooth, heart shaped one.

It looked like it might be cream filled. He lifted it to her mouth, and watched in enjoyment as she bit into it, her lips lush and full, enjoyment apparent in her eyes.

She closed her eyes as she took the full chocolate from his fingertips, and when her mouth closed, it was all he could do not to lean in and taste any sugar that was left on his lips. He watched her savor the sweetness, and when she opened her eyes, she smiled.

"Heaven," she breathed.

They were quiet for a moment, again lost in each other's eyes. She leaned forward towards him, and delivered a soft kiss on his cheek.

"Thank you for cheering me up," she whispered in his ear.

Pulling gracefully away, she stood. "I better go back into my room. The nurses will be looking for me."

Zeb stood as well. "Cassidy -- I want you to know something. I care about you. I'm beginning to -- to really care about you. If you need anything, day or night, please call me." He wrote his private cell phone number on the back of the gift shop receipt and handed it to her.

"You'll take care of me?" she asked. There was a hint of fear in her voice.

All he knew was that he wanted her to feel safe.

"I'll take care of you," he promised.

NINE

He rode his motorcycle away, feeling frustrated at the situation. All he wanted to do was kiss her, hold her, stroke her hair, and tell her that everything was going to be alright. But he had no right to touch her, or to hold her, and couldn't promise that she would be alright when in reality he had no idea if it was true. He shouldn't have said that he would take care of her. He did not know if it was in his power to save her from the risks of the surgery ahead.

Zeb didn't have a chance to visit Cassidy on Thursday. When he walked into work on Friday morning, he was immediately bombarded with Sondra's presence. Sondra, another resident in the neurosurgery program, often struck him as uptight and bossy. They had worked closely together for the past five years, and had become friends. He could look past her bossiness just as he was sure she'd learned to look past his know–it-all, blunt attitude.

"Did you hear?" Sondra asked, the moment Zeb rounded the corner and stepped onto North Nine. "The PKD girl is gone. Left AMA."

"What?" Zeb stopped in his tracks, his coffee lifted halfway to his mouth. "What do you mean, gone?"

"I mean she left. She asked for privacy last night, and then when the nurses went in to take vitals, she was gone. The nurses have looked everywhere, and even called her parents. They finally called back just a few minutes ago to say that arrived at home and they can't convince her to come back."

"PKD girl left against medical advice? Think she got cold feet?" asked Rohit, the third year resident asked, joining them.

Sondra shrugged. They'd all seen people lose it before surgery, especially one as risky as Cassidy's.

Jack joined the huddle. "What happened? I just heard about Cassidy Novotny. Zeb, what do you know?"

"Me?" Zeb feigned innocence.

"Oh please!" Sondra rolled her eyes. "We've all seen the way she looks at you Zeb. You're the reason she's here."

"If any of us are going to convince her to come back, it's you," agreed Jack.

"I don't think I should --"protested Zeb. He stopped midsentence. He was thinking about Cassidy. If she didn't go in for surgery the next morning, she was giving up on the best chance she had at survival. What was she thinking? How come she hadn't called him?

Did she even care about him at all?

The group was looking at him, waiting for him to continue. He opened his mouth again, but closed it. He couldn't speak. His face felt flushed.

Jack pulled him aside. "What's going on?" Jack asked. "You doing okay with this?"

"I don't know. I think... I think I really like her, Jack."

"Well keep it in your pants," Jack warned crassly. "That's strictly against hospital policy. Once she's off our service, you two can have whatever kind of relationship you want to. Sondra's right, we've all seen the way you guys look at each other. The girl's head over heels, and you're practically drooling."

"She has a boyfriend," said Zeb. This was the first time he had spoken about his feelings for Cassidy outloud, and he was reeling with the confirmation that others could sense the tension between them. He hadn't been sure if he was merely imagining their chemistry, but his whole team seemed to have noticed it. He wasn't making it up. They had something.

Then why was she with someone else?

"Some guy up in Montreal, who she's been with for five years."

Jack shrugged, "Just because they've stayed together for a long time doesn't mean that he's right for her."

"But Jack, she's our patient. I shouldn't even be --"

Jack cut him off. "Zeb, sometimes you can't help how you feel. These things happen."

Jack should know, thought Zeb. He'd fallen for his intern, and that was 'strictly against hospital policy' itself.

"I knew when I met her, that I had feelings for her. I mean the instant I looked at her, Jack. I shouldn't have been on this case. I should have said something."

"Look, Zeb, I think you have this all wrong. It's *good* that you met her, and *good* that you're her doctor. You're already saved her life once. Maybe this is about more than removing an aneurism. Maybe she needs more help than that. Do you think you can get her back in here? Call her and try to talk some sense into her? She seems to trust you."

"I can try."

Jack nodded. He looked as if he was thinking something over. He took out his notebook and looked it over, avoiding Zeb's eyes as he continued in a business-like tone."If she's not in by nine pm, and prepping for surgery, we've got to get another one going. Hart is too in demand to leave his schedule open, and she can't have surgery unless she's here, not eating and drinking. So nine pm. Got it?"

Zeb nodded, already planning out what he would say.

"You're needed in the OR in fifteen. You'll call her first?"

"I will."

"Page us if you get through," ordered Jack, and rushed away.

Zeb took out his phone, dialing her number, which he now had programmed in as 'tiara girl', because of the feeling it brought up in him. He loved to remember the night they met.

It went straight to voicemail. He imagined her in her favorite blanket, eating chocolates and forgetting that the world existed. Of course she wouldn't pick up a call from him, a reminder of the challenges that lay ahead of her, the stark reality of her diagnosis. Even if they successfully repaired the aneurism, that was only removing the ticking time bomb. The enemy was still very much intact, lying in wait in her kidneys. It was only a matter of time before she developed more aneurysms -- unless she received a kidney transplant. Yes, she had an uphill battle in front of her; this was only the preliminaries. Was she ready for the fight? Her leaving against medical advice didn't say anything good about her mental state.

He left a voicemail, his voice hard and strained as he fought to find a balance between her doctor and the friend that he had found himself becoming.

"We need you back here by nine pm the latest, Cassidy," he said, after explaining the situation and the reason he was calling, "Or else your opportunity is gone.

Hart is booked far in advance. This is your shot at recovery -- at life, Cassidy. Please call me back."

If she didn't want to fight for her own life, he wasn't sure that he could fight for her.

His anger built as he ran down the hospital stairs towards the OR, now late. He felt like he was on an emotional roller coaster. He had only just been elated to know that his team could sense the chemistry between he and Cassidy, but now he felt distinctly angry at her. His thoughts began to get darker as he ran towards the OR. Memories of his life with his mother bubbled up uncontrollably.

He'd been fighting for himself and his mom for so long. Yet, no matter what he did, she had refused to fight with him, to better herself or their situation.

She just kept drinking, he thought, pushing the stairwell doors open and stepping out into the corridor, *and now look at her*. She didn't even recognize him; her own son. He slowed to a walk now that he was out in public. Nurses and orderlies streamed past him, on their way to the ER or ICU. He turned left towards the OR.

He was thinking about the day they had found out about the dimensia. His mother had been found naked, asleep by a nearby apartment complex's hot tub. Someone had called the police, and they brought her to the ER. After many tests, the doctors said that alcohol had exacerbated the early onset Dimensia, increasing her risk for the disease that was a part of her genetic makeup. But Zeb harbored a deep seeded belief that the drinking had caused it.

And now Cassidy was pulling the same thing: Making him feel like he was responsible for her life, but taking no responsibility herself. Sabotaging any hope of recovery that she had. He knew that it was a mistake, allowing himself to feel what he did. But he couldn't help it. She was using the same old victim mentality that he saw in his mom. He'd worked hard on Cassidy's case, as her doctor. He'd given her all he could: his personal time, his care and attention. She was throwing away her shot.

He saw it time and again. He tried to fix people, but some of them refused to fix themselves. And that was what they needed to do. He couldn't do that for them.

He shot Jack a page before scrubbing into the first of many scheduled surgeries, letting him know that his attempt had failed.

Someone else would have to try.

She didn't pick up, he texted.

The OR was stressful, and he was glad to leave once five o'clock hit.

He found himself driving his motorcycle towards the beachfront address that he'd seen on her paper work: her parent's house.

He drove until he saw it, 64 Frontview , a beautiful white house with a picket fence. He walked up to the gate, unlatched it, following his senses. He could guess that the stone walkway wrapping around the back of the house would lead to the guest cabin. He was right.

He stepped up to the door, lifted his fist, and knocked. She had three and a half hours before Jack would give her OR time away to someone else. He had to be back for his on-call shift by nine as well. Despite his feeling that she was throwing away his hard work, he still wanted to save her. His anger had fueled a senseless determination in him. He wasn't returning without her.

TEN

The girl that opened the door was not the same one that he'd left at the hospital. He'd expected to see her in a puddle of exhaustion or depression, crumpled tissues around her, a blanket wrapped around her. He'd expected desperation, grief, fear. But he was met with a beautiful girl in a pink dress. She was showered, her hair washed, and that damn sexy eyeliner, heavy on her lids, lilting high up on the edges. Her eyelashes were thick. She smiled at him, opened the door wider.

"Oh, I am so glad you are here!" she greeted him.

Is she insane? he wondered. *Has she regressed into total denial?*

She was acting as if she was normal, like she hadn't fled the hospital earlier that day. As if she didn't have a life or death surgery scheduled for the morning.

"Cassidy, what are you doing?" He couldn't hide the anger in his voice. "A lot of people have been working hard to treat your condition, and you throw it all away? What kind of a thanks is that?" He'd meant it for the whole team, but it came out sounding as if he was only concerned for himself.

Cassidy eyed her hot doctor. She wanted to eat him up, like a chocolate bar. She put out her hand, pulled him in, opening the door wider. He was speaking, she was

68

aware, but she wasn't listening. She was only focused on him, on how handsome he was, and what a perfect date he made.

Margo and Marcus's wedding was tonight, and she refused to miss it. Her life had been morphing into something she barely recognized. She'd needed a shower and her own soaps an lotions and yes, to wrap up in a blanket and be left in peace on the couch. She had used the time to order her thoughts, and to take care of some things. Like Evan. She'd finally called him, and told him everything. Not only about her diagnosis, and the surgery, but that she didn't want to continue on with him. That it was over between them. It was a lot to say over the phone, but he'd handled it surprisingly well. She felt a million times lighter once she'd delivered the news.

This might be her last day on earth. She could not spend it in that hospital room.

She had reasoned her way through it, and when Zeb left her the message about returning by nine o'clock, she realized that she could stay away from the hospital for the day. She had been given the gift of time, and she sorely needed it. A day of her own, away from tests, measurements, charts, and orders. A luxurious day to pretend that she was normal.

Once she'd gotten the break-up with Evan over and done with, she'd taken a long, hot shower. She'd dressed and gone out for a walk on the lake, enjoying the expanse of blue water like she'd never seen it before. The way the light hit the rippling waves, the way the trees wavered in the wind, it was all so heartbreakingly beautiful. She'd never noticed before. *Really* noticed. Not like this.

She felt alive.

That afternoon, she'd baked cupcakes with her mother, enjoying and noticing the smell of her mother's sweater, even the soft way her dad spoke, the way he looked at her. All these things that she'd taken for granted her entire life, she was noticing now.

She was *seeing* the man before her. He was so alive, so full of good intention. He only wanted to help her; she could see that clearly. Even his anger was well intentioned. She could see that he didn't know that she would return to the hospital tonight. She wasn't giving up this fight. She just had to take the time that she was given, incase this was the end.

Maybe he didn't understand that; being as healthy as he was. He fixed other people, he'd never allowed himself to be fixed or cared for, it seemed. She pulled him along into the living room, picking a flower from the bouquet of wildflowers she'd collected that afternoon, and tucking one behind her ear.

She was in her bridesmaid's dress. Since she had left for Vermont straight from the airport, she found that most of the clothes she'd packed were vacation clothes, and she was excited to wear the beautiful, island-ready pink sun dress.

She led her hot doctor to the couch and settled him in with a drink of soda water, as she connected her laptop to Becky through Skype.

"Evan told us. How are you holding up?" Becky asked first thing once the connection had been made.

Cassidy was glad that she'd told Evan he could relay her news to their group of friends. She was slowly reconciling it in her own mind, but it was still hard to deliver to others.

"I'm good," said Cassidy, feeling the words reverberate in her chest with truth. She pointed the laptop screen to her couch companion, so that Becky could see him through the camera. "Becky, meet Zeb," she said.

Zeb waved, and then settled in even closer to Cassidy on the couch, getting a good view of the screen.

Becky was thrilled that Cassidy was well enough to them virtually. She started walking around with her iPad, showing her the venue and helping Cass facetime with their friends. They were waiting for Margo's entrance, and after a half an hour of this Becky started looking concerned.

The camera began to wobble erratically as Becky spotted something in the distance and hurried to it, apparently forgetting about her Skype companions.

"What's happening?" Cassidy wondered aloud.

Zeb was warm next to her. The old guest room couch caved in slightly in the middle and pushed them together. She was more than a little aware that he had placed one hand on her leg, as the sat close together on the couch. His touch felt warm and comforting. It delivered that safe, familiar, cared for feeling that she loved about him. She leaned into him, still watching the laptop screen intently. The screen showed palm trees at odd angles as Becky moved across the island resort, hurrying towards something.

Why was Margo late to her own wedding, after all of the planning that they'd done? The whole event seemed very removed from her life now, and she wasn't as concerned as she would have been had this been taking place before her diagnosis. But she was still curious to see find out what was happening.

The screen leveled, and she heard Becky's voice. "Margs? What's happening?"

They saw Margo was sitting on a white stone bench, bright orange tropical flowers blooming behind her as they weaved up a beautiful wooden lattice fence. She wore her wedding dress, a strapless white number with turquoise stones sewn into the neckline. Mascara was running down her face in wet tear streaks.

"What's wrong honey?" Cassidy heard Becky ask.

"It's Marcus. He's gone!"

"Don't be ridiculous!" There as a shuffling, and the iPad, apparently forgotten, was laid on the bench and showed a view of the clear, Dominican Republic sky. "He can't be gone. We're on an island! It's his wedding day. Where in the world would he go?"

"He left a-a-a—noooote," Margo's voice wailed and dissolved into more sobs.

"What does it say?" asked Cassidy though the computer. She was grateful that she was connected to her friend.

"It says, that he... that he feels 'trapped'. And that he felt like everyone expected too much from him, and that he couldn't handle the pressure. He went home."

Margo had picked up the iPad and was looking into the camera now.

"Cass? This is a disaster. I'm sorry to be so dramatic. You're literally facing -- life or-or-or deeeeaaaath." This brought on waterworks again.

Becky joined in. Now the two of them were crying.

"Come on, Becky," said Margot. "Let's go to her. Cass?"

"Yes?" asked Cassidy.

"We're coming to visit. We're taking care of this mess here and getting home to you."

Cassidy felt her heart well up. *Thank God*, she thought. She realized how much she needed her friends with her.

"Don't bring wine to the hospital," she joked. "They don't allow it."

"See you soon, honey," they signed off.

The screen went blank, and Cassidy felt herself begin to laugh. It was all so funny, from this new perspective, in which she might die the next day. All of this drama, all of the tears and the fighting and the yelling, and even the love, was like a big, beautiful circus. She laughed harder, and harder, until tears were streaming down her eyes. She heard Zeb let out a chuckle next to her.

She leaned into him, and felt his arms wrap around her. She couldn't stop laughing, and she felt his body shake with laughter too. She felt like he was *getting* it. What this was all about. How wonderful and mad it all was, all of this chaos -- all of this life, all around them.

Her laughter died down, and she looked at him. She leaned forward, watching his face, and kissed him. When her lips touched his, it was like she was melting into him. She felt as if she was finally safe; as if this was the one place in the world that she was truly meant to be; as if she could die tomorrow, and still she would feel complete.

She felt him return the kiss, moving his lips in tandem with hers, tasting her mouth like it was something he'd hungered for. She felt him draw her into him, his strong arms encapsulating her with the strength that she'd been dreaming of ever since he had held her on the first night they met.

She felt herself warm against him, a flower opening to the sun. She pulled away from the kiss and looked at him, just enjoying the way his eyes sparked into hers. All else faded, and she was his. He smiled, and she moved a hand to touch the dimple that creased his cheek. She moved her hands along his face, exploring every inch of his jaw line and tracing a line down his neck, finding his collar and then laying her hands on his chest. He closed his eyes, and she could tell that he needed her touch as much as she needed him. With her hands on his chest, she felt as if she was giving him the same gift that he gave her -- the feeling of being cared for.

He sighed, and she felt him let his body relax deeper into the couch, moving into a more horizontal position. She fell with him, pressed into him. Now her body was on top of his, and she enjoyed every inch of the contact that they now had. She loved the firmness of his torso, the way his muscles flexed when he moved his arms to hold her. She loved the smell of him; clean and spicy, like aftershave. She breathed in, letting her hand drift along his arm as he held her. Her hand tucked in between his bicep and tee-shirt sleeve, and she left it there as she found his lips again.

They were perfect lips, and he was a wonderful kisser. He met her mouth with tenderness, drawing her deeper into him as their kiss grew deeper. His tongue played along hers, and she felt him grow hard and move his body against hers.

The sensations were wonderful; more than she could have asked for. She wanted to enjoy every moment of this encounter to the maximum.

"Chocolate," she murmured, smiling as she pulled herself upward, and she saw Zeb catch his breath. She found what she was looking for. She lifted the piece of chocolate cupcake on a fork, and held it forward towards him. He smiled as he sat up a bit on the couch. His hair was roughed up, standing straight up in the front. His tee shirt was wrinkled, and he looked happy. He moved his

mouth towards the fork, meeting her eyes as he bit the
cake off, licking his lips.

"Now you," she said. "It's your turn to feed me."

"Gladly," he said, reaching for the fork.

"Not here," she said. "Come with me." She wanted
more of him. She wanted all of him. She picked up the
cake in one hand and led him with the other into her
bedroom.

He paused in the doorway, eyeing her.

She loved the way his eyes couldn't help but wander
down her body. She knew that her body looked good in
the tight pink sundress. It highlighted all of her curves, in
all the right ways. His eyelids were hooded, and he looked
like he could barely contain the desire that he felt for her,
although he seemed to be trying. She couldn't help going
to him, kissing him fervently, enjoying his hungry kisses in
return. She ran her hands through his hair, something
she'd wanted to do since their first meeting.

And then she took her heels off, one at a time, and
climbed onto the bed. She knelt in the middle of the bed,
feeling wonderfully sexy in her sundress that she knew
was giving him an eyeful of her cleavage as she leaned
forward.

She let her tongue travel lightly around her mouth,
and saw that this had his rapt attention. "Here," she said,
handing him the fork.

"Cassidy, wait," he said, and she could tell that it was
a struggle for him to talk. "Are you sure, that this is what
you want?"

"I've never been more sure of anything in my life," Cassidy said, wonderfully clear. *Thinking about death has a way of doing that*, she thought. Everything seemed to magically be in the right perspective.

He walked towards her, and she concentrated so that she would never forget a second of the way she felt as he approached her. She loved the sight of him -- his rough good looks contrasting the white innocence of the guest cabin's decorations. She loved the way his body looked in the black tee shirt stretched tightly over his rippling muscles. She liked it almost as much as she enjoyed seeing him in his scrubs and white coat.

This thought reminded her of the surgery, tomorrow. She wanted to feel everything tonight, before it might be too late. She did not want to go into surgery without taking this chance. She couldn't.

He climbed up on to the bed, nearly pushing her over as he found her lips again, his hands cupping her face and his kisses short but deep. She let him kiss her, and lean down to the top of her breasts, lightly kissing her there as well.

She then placed the cake between them, and he lifted a forkful to her mouth. She licked her lips, knowing that what she wanted now was more than chocolate, more than sweetness, more than cake. She wanted him. She let her hands reach for him, and as she placed her mouth on the fork, she reached for his belt buckle.

Slowly pressing her lips onto the fork, watching her eyes and letting her lips pull the food from the extended prongs, she watched his desire growing steadily hotter as she unzipped his pants, and slid her hand inside.

He was hard, bigger than she'd hoped, firm and throbbing with desire. She felt the shaft, stroking lightly, licking her lips again. She used one hand to remove some icing from the cake and she placed it on her finger. She moved this to his mouth, and let him suck on her finger as she stroked him with the other hand. She leaned forward and kissed the chocolate from his lips, savoring the way he tasted and felt. Leading him to the edge of the bed, she helped him stand, and moved herself down, down, pulling his pants along with her, and placing her lips there. She sucked on his throbbing member, feeling the heady thrill of control as he moaned and stroked her hair. She felt alive; wonderfully so.

"Cassidy," he murmured. "I want to..." he was lost again in a moan of ecstasy as she swirled her tongue around him. And then he pulled her up, eyeing her as if he could not control himself any longer. He turned her around, unzipping the back of her dress, letting his hands slide along her back, lifting her hair and kissing her neck as he unzipped her.

He had pulled his own tee shirt off, and now she felt him press against her skin. The feel of his skin next to hers was almost too much to bear. He bent himself around her, peeling the dress down as he pressed into her, kissing her neck as he did so.

The dress fell to the floor.

She was braless, and his hands found her breasts. She loved the feel of his hands on her breasts, toying gently with her nipples, which hardened at his touch..

She turned, finding his mouth, kissing him hungrily once again.

He broke away, and she watched him reach for the cake, and lift dark icing onto his finger. Her anticipation grew as placed icing on each breast, and then licked it off with his tongue. The sight of his tongue on her body, and the feel of him sucking on her nipple sent waves of desire through her.

His mouth moved down her body, and she felt his hands stroking her through the satin underwear she wore. Knowing that she could not last much longer without the feel of him inside of her, she moved to the bedside table and found a condom, placed it on him before finding his hand and guiding it between her legs again. She was warm with desire and need.

The way he rubbed her sent shrill shocks of need jolting up her core. He slid a finger in first, parting her, and she could feel the warmth and wetness quivering against his finger. Finally, he moved her onto the bed, and entered her.

He was slow and tender, and she savored the feeling of the length of him penetrating deeply into her. He kissed her mouth as he moved, slowly, gently, every inch of her aching with the bliss of his hardness inside of her. He reached for the cake, and she tasted chocolate icing as he moved his finger to her mouth. The sweetness, the movement, the bliss she was experiencing, was unlike anything she'd ever known.

When she felt him quake with release, she came along with him, bliss and ecstasy completely overwhelming her.

Afterward, they both lay on the bed, holding each other, not wanting to interrupt the feeling of bliss that was lingering around them.

It was nearly a half an hour before Cassidy pulled herself up. "Now, we should go back to the hospital, Doctor Morgan."

He could see that she was being facetious, but the words jolted him unpleasantly back to reality. What had he just done? He would be operating on this woman tomorrow.

That's why I did this, he realized. He couldn't let her pass from this world without letting her feel just how much he cared for her. He pushed aside any unpleasantness that came with her words, and forced himself to think of what it was like to be her -what it would feel like to know that the world might end within twenty four hours.

He leaned forward and kissed her. "You're right." He glanced at his watch. "And we'd better hurry." It was twenty to nine.

He reached for his cell phone and texted Jack: *Cassidy is on her way. Don't give the spot away*

He was relieved when a text came back in.

Nice job man, it said. *I'll let the team know.*

He realized that they had no idea what he had done, and it better stay that way.

ELEVEN

Later that evening, back in the hospital, Cassidy fought to keep the clarity that she'd experienced during the day. She was trying to sleep, but it was impossible.

She couldn't stop thinking about life and death, huge subjects that she somehow had managed to ignore for her first twenty seven years on the planet. How had she been so blissfully ignorant? How had she never even considered dying? She'd assumed that she would live into old age, and the thought that she wouldn't never crossed her mind. Until now.

Now, it held a permanent position in her mind, like a blinking sign, flashing on a billboard; incessant, unceasing, relentless.

At least with Zeb around she could have her mind on other things.

Like the way he made her feel. Special. Loved. Needed. Cherished.

She heard the door to her hospital room open, and looked up. It was Zeb.

"Oh thank God," she said. "I'm going down a negative spiral in here."

"I thought you might be," he said.

"You guys busy tonight?"

Zeb shrugged, seeming to not want to worry her with news of the hospital. "The usual," he said. "More importantly, how is my favorite patient doing?"

"Trying not to be scared. Trying not to think too much. It's hard."

He had closed the door behind him. He looked like he was up to something; his hands were behind his back. He carefully drew the curtain around her bed. She heard him slide something around.

"What is happening?" she asked, in happy anticipation of a surprise. Maybe he'd brought her something from the gift store. Maybe it was a cute stuffed animal holding a heart, or a bouquet of flowers. Whatever it was, he was being awfully sneaky about it.

The curtain remained closed. She heard music start, chords to a song she recognized. It was slow, sultry, sexy. She saw his hand on the curtain.

Before he pulled it back, she heard him say. "And now, welcome the Magic Medical Maverick! World's all time best stripper. Here for the distinct entertainment of Ms. Casssiiidyy Novotny!!" He stretched out her name, long and slow so that he sounded like a cheesy sports announcer.

She laughed aloud.

The song picked up, and Zeb came into the space within the curtain. He was dancing, exaggeratedly, around her. He did slow circles, and was undoing the buttons of his coat. She caught a glimpse of his bare chest beneath his white coat.

"Tell me you didn't...!" she said, as she noticed for sure that he wore no top beneath his jacket.

He let the coat fall onto her bed. She could not believe what was happening. *I must be dreaming*, she thought, laughing.

She glanced to the door, afraid that a nurse might come in. They seemed to come in often, to check on this or that. It made it very difficult to get any sleep.

Zeb had placed a table against the door, blockading it from the inside.

She laughed out loud again.

"It's just us, sugar baby," he said, in what she suspected must be an attempt at a sexy voice. Instead it just came out funny, and she put a hand over her mouth to stifle a laugh.

God, it felt great to laugh. Her emotion surged into her throat, and she almost cried at the same time that she was laughing. *How did I ever take this for granted before?* she wondered, of the feeling that was bubbling up inside of her like a happy brook. It was so uncontrollable, so delicious.

He was really getting into it, gyrating his hips and swinging his jacket around over his head. He put it between his legs and brought it back and forth. He turned around and stuck his butt into the air, and started pushing it towards her.

"What is happening?" she asked, between fits of giggles. "Someone help me! I don't know if this is a strip tease or a seizure!"

"That's right baby," he said, now laughing along with her. "That's my style. You will never forget it." He reached for something off of a side table, and walked towards her. She gasped when she saw what it was. The tiara she'd worn on the night that they met.

He'd saved it.

Had he known that she was something special, that night? Like she'd known it? The thought made her light headed.

"Get ready to be so wowed that you won't be able to contain yourself."

He danced some more and then untied his scrub pants.

"Stop!" she cried. "Stop." She was looking at the door again. "You're crazy! You're going to get fired, Doctor Morgan."

He laughed. "For you, Cassidy, I'd get fired. It's worth it to see you laugh."

"Can I get a lap dance?" she joked, once she saw he wasn't really going to take his pants off.

"I don't want to risk hurting you," he said. "I'm kind of an amateur. I probably couldn't tell because of the mad skill of my moves, but..."

"Then a kiss. How much for a kiss?"

"You can't buy this," he said, waving his finger through the air like a diva.

"Come one. One? I'll give you my tiara."

"Well, alright."

He sat down on the bed with her and leaned forward. He still had his shirt off. She placed her hands on his bare chest and looked him in the eyes. And there he was: Zeb. The man who cared about her. She gave up the act, and kissed him for real.

It felt so good to make her laugh. To take away some of her suffering. All he wanted was to make her feel better.

"I'll take care of you." he said. It felt so good to see the trust in her face, the relief that came over her, as if she truly believed that he had the power to save her. "You are going to be fine, Cassidy Novotny", he said, holding her in a hug.

He wanted, more than anything, for his words to be true.

TWELVE

"I want you to be the first person I see, when I wake up," she whispered the next morning, when they had a moment alone behind the curtain. She was now in pre-op, and Zeb knew that there were just minutes before Dr. Hart, Doctor Wineright, Jack and he would be operating.

"I want that too," he replied. He was anxious as hell, but he tried his best to ignore his jangling nerves. He didn't allow himself to think about the things he was feeling for the woman who had turned his life upside down.

The OR was cold and sterile. Zeb could feel his heart pounding. Music was playing, the oldies that Hart liked. That calmed him a little. Not the music-- he could take it or leave it-- but the familiarity of the scene, and knowing that Hart was skilled and that this was just another day in the office for him.

Not the most important day of his life.

Doctor Hart wasn't operating on a woman he.... had, feelings for? What were the feelings? Zeb and Cassidy had moved so quickly beyond friendship that Zeb didn't even know what to label their relationship in his mind. He couldn't even think about it now.

Luis sedated Cassidy, an airway was secured, her eyes taped over and a sterile blue cloth placed over her body and around her head, with a window at the back of her skull. Pre-op had shaved a space for them, and this was sterilized and prepped. Jack made the first incisions.

Zeb could see that Jack was taking over some of the duties that usually he would delegate to Zeb. There seemed to be a mutual understanding between them. Jack seemed to understand that his feelings for this patient in particular had moved beyond normal. They didn't say it in so many words, and he knew that the whole team was glad that she was back in the hospital, not walking around Burlington with a quarter sized aneurysm in her head. She needed help, and they wanted to give it. Jack didn't ask how their conversation had gone, how he'd convinced her to return, and Zeb did not share any details.

But he'd been thinking about them.

With the initial incisions, injections, and sterilizations completed, a surgical saw was used to remove a part of her skull. Once they had the brain opened, the cameras were inserted, and the operation was enlarged on two expansive computer monitors at the head of the bed. As Dr. Wineright manipulated the controllers as if he was playing a videogame, Zeb saw in detail the inside of Cassidy's brain.

"There," said Hart, seeing something that no one else did, as usual. "That purple engorged formation to the left. Follow it."

Zeb hadn't even seen any abnormalities. There was a reason Hart was the best of the best; he had a sixth sense when it came to brains.

Wineright turned the micro camera and embedded it farther into a crevasse in the dural matter. They could see her blood vessels now, and it was apparent that one was growing in size the deeper that they travelled. This was their culprit. The tools dug farther in, farther, until they found the balloon-like aneurism. The weakened vessel wall was pulsating with blood, and the sack was glistening, alive, and looked very dangerous.

"Far to big for coiling," muttered Hart. "We were right about that. A number two should work. If we angle it like this," he motioned to the left of the ballooning vessel, "It won't interfere with this flow here." He motioned with his gloved hand again as the rest of them nodded, looking at the screen.

"I'll get clips ready," Zeb spoke. A nurse brought him a tray of clips in all sizes. He chose a number two as well as a number three, in case the first option didn't work. More tools were prepared and Wineright placed expanders around the vessel.

"It's fragile," noted Jack, as more of it was exposed.

Hart nodded. "It's a miracle that she came in when she did."

Jack looked to Zeb pointedly as Hart spoke these words.

Zeb felt light-headed.

Jack was given the expanders, and asked Zeb to lavage the area, which Zeb did, still forcing himself to not think about the fact that he was looking inside Cassidy's skull. Hart inserted the titanium micro clip. The number two was too small but the number three fit perfectly.

They reconstructed the blood flow and strengthened the vessel near the clip with synthetic mesh, ensuring that the clipping wouldn't cause any new weak areas that would then burst. The repair and closure of the window took another two hours, and by the time the surgery was over, Zeb felt absolutely spent. He knew that Cassidy would go into post op for the rest of the day as she came out of anesthesia, and then would go into the

ICU. If all went well, she could be discharged by the end of the week.

And then what? he wondered.

Would she return to Montreal? Would he see her again? She still had the kidney disease to deal with. Would she get treatments in Vermont, or go back to Canada? Would she want to return to her normal life, school, her friends, her apartment, and forget all about him?

Suddenly Luis spoke up, and Zeb was jerked out of his wonderings.

"Respiratory rate is eight," Luis said. "Heart rate 33."

Doctor Hart motioned to Jack and Zeb. "Get it sewn up, she's been exposed. Her bodies fighting the re-route," Hart said.

Zeb didn't like the strain in his voice, the urgency. *This isn't over yet*, he reminded himself.

"Zeb, push three mcg of benzapine," Wineright ordered. He did and gave it to the OR nurse, turning to the OR nurse who was charting so that they could see it. He pushed it through the IV line and saw her blood pressure come back up slightly.

But then her blood pressure sank down again, and her heart rate plummeted. "Three more!" Wineright ordered, and Zeb rushed to pull it up. He wasn't thinking about anything now, he'd gone into surgeon mode and was handling his orders confidently and efficiently. He could only think of saving her. The future wouldn't matter if she wasn't a part of it.

Finally her circulation was stable again, but Hart shook his head. "I don't like it," he said. "She shouldn't have vasodialated like that. Her arterial system is not recognizing the new flow. We need to monitor her closely.

Call me at the clinic if it happens again. It might mean that we have to do an additional intervention."

Zeb felt uneasy as they rolled her into post op. Her face was swollen, pale, and clammy. She looked lifeless, and he was afraid to leave her. But he had to. He had other patients to see, as well as a full OR schedule. He couldn't stay with her. He pulled a nurse aside and asked her to page him immediately when she awoke.

By six pm, Zeb had scrubbed out of the OR suite. He'd been operating all day, but checking his beeper frequently, and had told his superiors that he had an emergent case that he had to check on if paged. Jack agreed and Zeb was ready to dash. But they hadn't called. Finally he couldn't stand it. *Why isn't she awake yet?* he worried. Every person handled anesthesia differently, and there was no predictable outcome, but it certainly was rare for a patient to sleep so long.

He entered post op and looked frantically around.

Spotting the nurse he had spoken to earlier about leave for the evening, he cornered her, blocking her exit. She looked frightened by his frantic body language.

"Where is she?" he demanded. "Cassidy Novotney. I told you to page me when she woke up!"

She backed away from him.

"I -- she didn't wake up. I notified neuro. Wineright came to see her. He said you were in the OR and not to bother you. She --"

"What do you mean she didn't wake up?"

"She wasn't clearing the anesthesia."

"She didn't wake up, but she's not here?"

"She slipped into a coma. Her respiratory rate was dropping. She had to go onto a re-breather..."

Zeb was pushing a hand through his hair, turning away from the nurse and pulling out his hand-held. He logged into the system to see the latest. He was angry, but knew he shouldn't direct it at the nurse.

"I'm sorry," he said, scrolling quickly through the patient lists, "I shouldn't be yelling at you. She had surgery this morning and I need to follow up."

"Wineright said to put her on seizure precautions, re-breather, and post- op coma protocol. She was transferred two hours ago, after we --"

Oh God. In two hours, anything could have happened.

He left the nurse before she could finish her report, running towards the ICU.

The ICU was crowded, and there was activity around Cassidy's bed. The nurses were hooking up monitors to her heart and pushing buttons on her re-breather. She was being administered a treatment through the machine to help her lungs stay clear while she was unconscious. Because she'd been in surgery and could not take deep breaths on her own, Zeb knew that pneumonia was one of her risk factors. Her face was still puffy, her eyes like two pale slits. She was as lifeless as earlier.

The visuals were worse than the words. He couldn't look at her like that. It was his worst fear, seeing her like this. He'd prayed that the surgery would go well, but now she wasn't waking up. They had done their job, but her body was repelling the fix, fighting it, and she wasn't recovering.

She was getting worse. Would she make it?

He couldn't look at her. He turned away, and one of the nurses came to him and started talking, as if he was there to give more orders. This was logical on the nurse's part, but the last thing he felt like doing was trying to present himself as a capable doctor at that moment. He felt afraid. . He felt he had given everything he had. Speechless, he looked at the nurse and then back to Cassidy. He mumbled something about a call he'd forgotten to make, and turned. All he could manage to do, in order to retain his professional composure at that moment, was walk away.

He went to the locker room, and changed. Then, he walked out into the night. He passed the bench that they had sat on, and sank into it, pretending that she was there next to him. He could hear her soft, sweet voice in his ear; he could see those eye, how on fire they'd been just the night before, as they'd made love.

She'd asked him to be there when she woke up.

He looked up at the night sky, searching the stars. She remembered her voice, when she had whispered in his ear that morning: 'I want you to be the first person I see, when I wake up.'

He had to go back in. For her.

That she wanted.

At least it would be easier now that he had changed. He would just have to explain that he was there on personal matters, not as her doctor. He turned and re-entered the hospital. He had to face his fear of seeing her so lifeless and helpless. He had to be strong. He wanted to be there for her. He wanted her to wake up.

He found a seat by her bed. The ICU never sleeps, but he was able to pull a curtain around them. He saw the gossip spreading; that he was here on his personal time, holding her hand. But he didn't care. He needed to be there.

What if she could hear him? He'd read cases of patients who could report on things that happened in surgery. *What if she is right here, in this room, not in her body?* he wondered. He knew that she, the woman he cared for, did not live in the brain that he had operated on. Then where was she?

"Cass?" he whispered. "Help me to be strong. I'm afraid, right now. For you, and for me. Because I think I'm falling for you." He said it so quietly, so softly, but felt a shiver run up his spine when he said the words. *Maybe that was her,* he thought.

Exhausted from his day, but unable to sleep, he spent the night in the chair, holding on to her hand, unwilling to let go.

The next day, he was supposed to work. He didn't know if he would be able to, but thought he had to try. Just as he was pouring a cup of coffee in the cafeteria, his phone rang. It was his mother's assisted living residency. He didn't pick up, and instead paid for his coffee. Finally, as he walked towards the locker room to change, he listened to the voicemail. The message was from his mother's doctor, who requested that he call back as soon as possible.

He sat down on a bench in the locker room, and dialed the assisted living center.

"Mr. Morgan? We have some unfortunate news for you, about your mother. Are you sitting down?"

He knew, in the pit of his stomach, what was coming. He'd had to deliver the news to families countless times, and he knew just the tone of the doctor's voice.

"Yes, I am sitting down."

"Your mother passed away early this morning. I'm so sorry."

The words were like a punch in the gut. He physically felt ill, and almost dropped the coffee from his hand.

Shaking, he managed to set it on the bench as he leaned forwards, speaking urgently into the phone. "How? I just visited her; she was healthy."

This was the last thing that he'd expected.

It made him briefly forget about Cassidy,

"It was suicide," the doctor said, pain in her voice as she broke the news to the deceased's only son.

Zeb dropped the phone. He didn't know what to do. He slid off of the bench, onto the floor, and leaned back against the lockers.

When the others started trickling in, they gave him space. Finally Sondra came and sat next to him.

"Is it Cassidy? I'm sorry Zeb." She put her hand on his shoulder. "I know she's in a coma. But she could come out of it, at any moment. Don't give up."

He felt himself shaking his head, nauseated at the thought of saying the words out loud. "My mom --" Zeb saw Sondra frown with confusion. He forced himself to get the words out. "My Mom committed suicide this morning."

Sondra leaned over him and hugged him, and the warmth of her compassion was what she needed to thaw some of the ice that had frozen him stiff. He melted a little, and for the first time since Cassidy's surgery, he started to cry. His breath came out in bursts. He was not used to crying, but he could not help it. Sondra helped him up and led him to an armchair. She called Jack over and in hushed voices they talked about what could be done.

Jack hired a taxi to take him to his mother's nursing home, and asked Zeb if here was family around that could help him.

"I need to do this alone," said Zeb, his heart heavy as his friends loaded him into the taxi cab.

Jack's leaned in to the door. "I'll check on you when I get out of here, okay man? I'll be over at your place. You're going to get through this, Zeb."

Zeb wasn't sure.

All he knew was that his mom had given up the fight, and for whatever reason, he felt like it was his fault.

Guilt pressed heavily on his chest, making him feel ill.

He'd promised Cassidy that she would be okay, and she wasn't. She wasn't waking up. How could he have asked her to get the surgery? Was all fo this his fault? Had he killed her?

"Call me, when... if..." Zeb wanted to know Cassidy's condition, but he didn't know how state his question. His voice died off, but Jack picked up on Zeb's train of thought and nodded.

"I will man, I will. You'll know when she pulls out of it." He stressed *when*, and Zeb was grateful that he hadn't used the word 'if' in its place.

"I don't know when I'll... there will be things to sort through, arrangements. I don't know when I will be able to come back to--"

"Don't worry about that," said Jack, hand firmly on his shoulder. "Take the time that you need."

As the taxi pulled away, Zeb wondered how much time he would need. Could time heal this? Could time take away the guilt he was feeling? Could he ever try to fix anyone, ever again?

THIRTEEN

Cassidy opened her eyes, and saw blurring, swimming lights and shapes. As they came into focus, she saw lips, a nose, eyes...and hair. Short dark hair. Evan's hair. He was smiling at her.

"She's opening her eyes!" he called out.

The words seemed warbled, like she was hearing things underwater. She tried to move her head, to see who he was talking to, and the moment she moved, her head pounded in response. She could feel her brain, and it felt swollen, as if it was too big for her skull. She moved her mouth, but could not speak. Her lips felt dry and her mouth parched. She tried to focus again. This time it was Becky's face; a broad smile.

"Cass? Margo, get the nurse! She's waking up! Cass? Can you hear me?"

A hand on hers.

Movement around her.

Margo's voice in the hallway, shouting for someone to come in.

A nurse was there, holding her hand now. Cassidy saw Margo, leaning over the bed. "You made it, honey, you made it. We were so worried about you. You're back."

"Can you squeeze my hand?" the nurse wanted to know. Cassidy exerted effort to squeeze down on the hand, and closed her eyes, concentrating fully on the movement of her muscles. It felt good to close her eyes against the painful light. She kept her head straight. Moving it caused too much pain and nausea.

"Good, good, now the other one?"

Cassidy managed to complete the exam, and soon she saw a doctor enter the room. His white coat brought images of Zeb into her mind. As her memories came flooding back to her, she looked around the room.

Where is he? she wondered.

 She couldn't wait to see him.

Margo, Becky, Evan, two nurses, and Doctor Pace were all there with her, asking her questions and watching her carefully.

"Where is...?"

"Dr. Morgan?" guessed Jack. The nurses looked at him questioningly."He's not here right now. He wanted to be," he rushed, noticing her expression sadden. "He had a family emergencey."

She fell back in the bed, sadness welling up inside of her. Her emotions were raw, and she was having trouble thinking straight. All she knew was that she'd wanted him to be there, but he wasn't.

FOURTEEN

Zeb was in his mom's old room when he saw the text from Jack come in.

Cassidy is awake.

He stood from his position at the bottom of his mother's closet. He'd been going through a box of photographs as he sat there on the floor. Pictures of himself as a child. He'd always tried to be strong for his mom, and it was like he was back in that place as he looked at the young boy in the photographs, trying to look so tough in the pictures. He'd tried so hard to help her.

He knew it wasn't his fault that she had suffered in her life, and that perhaps now she was free from her pain. Perhaps she was in a better place. He thought of Cassidy's version of heaven, and the corners of his mouth lifted in an almost-smile. His eyes were sore from crying. He squeezed them shut, titling his face up to the ceiling as he comprehended the text message.

She was awake.

She was alive.

She had wanted him there, when she awoke.

He had to see her.

He didn't know if he could be strong for her. He had no strength left. But he wanted to try.

He drove to the hospital and took the stairs two at a time to her room. It was crowded with people; not what he'd expected. They'd always had a private world. He didn't know what their relationship was, how to speak to her. Was he her doctor? Her boyfriend?

He wanted very much to go straight to her and apologize, sinking to his knees and taking her hand, to apologize and explain.

Her friends and parents were staring. There was the guy who had punched him. Evan. There were Becky and Margo, he knew them from the video chat.

And there was Cassidy.

God it felt good to see her awake. She was waiting for him to speak.

He couldn't. He couldn't say what he needed to say with all of these people around. He looked at the guests again.

"Could you all give us a moment?" Cassidy asked her friends, and one by one they left; Evan last.

"Cassidy," he said, finally approaching the bed. So much had happened in his life since the fun and games of their relationship.

Her surgery, her coma.

The fear of losing her.

The feeling of losing his mom.

He felt like a different person -- a person that didn't know how to act around her.

"I had some terrible news," he blurted out awkwardly, unsure how to share the reason he hadn't been at her side. "From my Mom's assisted living home. Apparently, she couldn't manage anymore... with her depression. She ended her life. Yesterday morning."

"Oh my God, Zeb," Cassidy's hand went to her mouth, her eyes widened, softened. He could tell that she wasn't angry at him.

"I'm sorry that I wasn't here when you woke up," he said, moving closer to her.

"I'm sorry too," she said, lifting her chin to look at him. She grimaced with the movement, and her hand went to her head. She squeezed her eyes shut. He could tell it took effort to speak, to move, and to even have her eyes open. She kept her eyes closed as she continued speaking, and her voice was hoarse as she forced the words out. "I put too much pressure on you. And now you're mom... Oh Zeb."

He didn't want to cry in front of her. He didn't want her to see his weakness. She had enough to deal with.

"I don't know if I'll be the best company for you," he managed to say. Or strong enough to take care of you as you recover." Zeb didn't know how he would take care of himself, let alone another person.

"You don't have to," she said, opening her eyes.

Cassidy was exhausted, and her head was throbbing. She didn't mean to hurt him. She saw as she spoke that her words seemed to hurt him, and that was the last thing she meant to do. She just wanted him to know that he wasn't responsible for her. He had enough to deal with; to heal from. "I don't mean that in a bad way, Zeb. I mean, you don't have to save me. I'm getting discharged, soon. You're not my doctor anymore."

The words, even if they were meant to relieve his burden, made him feel even worse.

"You did everything for me Zeb. You saved my life. I'm thankful. I know I have a lot to get through still, but that's not your responsibility. You aren't responsible for me. You aren't responsible for your Mom. Do you understand?"

He wanted to cry. Damn, she would make a good psychologist. He felt like a child, like the boy in the photographs. Someone was finally telling him that it wasn't his fault. The knot of guilt that had grown in his heart felt loosened. He felt himself breathe. He took her hand.

"Is this goodbye?" he asked, not wanting it to be true.

"I'm going back to Montreal to finish the semester. I'm leaving tomorrow. I think you should take care of yourself right now, Zeb."

He nodded. He knew that she was right. He was in no place to be helping her recover, and she was in no place to help him. They both needed to heal for themselves.

He bent down and kissed her forehead, and she held his hands tightly. He saw a tear slide down her cheek. Finally he forced himself to turn and leave.

FIFTEEN

Christmas lights were up on Burlington's pedestrian main street, even though Thanksgiving had just passed. Zeb tucked a scarf around his neck, wishing he'd worn his winter coat instead of his leather jacket. An icy wind whipped off of the lake.

"Chocolate?" asked a female voice.

Zeb whipped around. The Lake Champlain Chocolates employee held out a silver, doily covered tray of gourmet chocolate samples.

Zeb nodded, choosing one carefully as the girl looked at him oddly. He guessed that he'd turned around a little too quickly. He'd just thought...something about her voice reminded him....

He let the chocolate melt on his tongue.

The funeral was over, and he was back at work. He felt his old self returning, the smart-ass rebel that made people laugh and always said things bluntly. His friends had been glad to have him back. He was glad to *be* back.

But often, at night before falling asleep, he thought about her. He picked up his phone and started composing a text or dialing her number, but then thought about what he was doing. What would he say? Was he ready to open himself up? To let himself care? Did she even want that?

He recognized a woman on the street; she was a nurse from his mother's assisted living home. She stopped him as he walked by, recognizing him as well.

"You're Ms. Morgan's son, aren't you?" she asked. "You know your Mamma went on and on about you?"

Zeb shook his head. He knew that his mom had trouble remembering him when she saw him, so he doubted that the nurse's stories were true. She was probably just trying to be kind.

"She was always clearest in the mornings," the nurse said, "when I was brushing her hair. Something about that always brought her back. One day I was brushing and she looked at me and said she had the most fearless boy. Wouldn't let anything or anybody hold him down. A 'go getter' she called you." She smiled at him.

"Said you put yourself through college and med school, with out a dime of help from anybody. Yep, a real go getter. So what've you been gone getting?"

Zeb was taken aback from the question.

Suddenly, he knew what he wanted to go and get.

He smiled at the woman. "Thank you," He said. You just reminded me of something," he saw her shake her head smiling as he turned away. He rushed to his car. How could he have been such an idiot?

He drove across the border into Montreal. Using his phone, he found the address for The Sweet Life, La Belle Vie. He hoped that she would be there.

A bell on the door tinkled as he opened it. The shop was crowded, every surface filled with jars of jelly beans and tiered shelves of elaborate toffees and caramels, swirling lollypops, glistening sugar coated treats of all colors, shapes and sizes. But mostly, there was chocolate -- housands of chocolates. He smiled. It was just how he had imagined it; the perfect place for the sweetest girl he'd ever met to work.

There was a bell on the counter, and a white card next to it. 'Ring for service', it instructed, and he gave it a tap, listening as the melodic tone chimed throughout the store.

He heard movement coming from the back room.

Suddenly, she was there, in front of him. Her hair was tucked under a hat, and she wore her dark eyeliner and a pink apron. His heart pounded at the sight of her. She was just as he remembered; even prettier.

She recognized him immediately.

He smiled. She rushed around the counter and wrapped her arms around his neck.

"I hope you're not here to give me another diagnosis," she whispered in his ear. "I've had enough of those for a lifetime, Doctor Morgan."

"No," he smiled. "It's me who has an illness this time."

She pushed him back, looking quizzically at him, unsure if he was joking.

He smiled, "I'm love sick. I'm love sick over a girl who got away. I need to get her back."

"Me?" she asked, folding back into his arms.

"You. My tiara girl." He found her lips and kissed her. It was kiss with no reservations.

She pulled away and looked at him. "I think I know just the remedy," she said, and leaned closer.

"I love you, Doctor Morgan."

He cupped her face in his hands. "I love you, Cassidy." It felt so wonderful to say the words.

"Becky, you didn't," Cassidy didn't know whether to laugh or grimace. She was relieved when she heard Margo laugh at her side.

"I love it!" Margo said.

Cassidy breathed out with relief. She'd once again been unable to help with the party planning, and Becky had taken matters into her own hands. She'd transformed her apartment into an island get away, complete with sandy floors, a tiki bar, and steel drums playing in the background.

"I figured since you said it was your dream to be married with your bare feet in the sand..."

Margo hugged Becky. "It's perfect. You even turned up the heat didn't you?"

"Well we are wearing sundresses in the middle of March, in Montreal. There's three feet of snow outside! I cranked it up to eight-five."

Cass slipped the silver over wrap off of her shoulders.

"You're brilliant." Margo declared, moving forward to check on the drinks.

"Bold move," laughed Cassidy.

"I checked with Marcus first, and he said it was a good idea," shrugged Becky. "This way, we get to have our destination wedding. Right here in Montreal."

"How is treatment going?" Margo asked, returning to them with a fruity cocktail in her hand.

"Great," Cass replied. "They say I don't need a transplant. The cysts are getting smaller with the medication and laser treatment."

"Thank goodness," said Margo.

"More importantly...." grinned Becky, "How is your smokin' hot doctor?"

"He's not my doctor any more," laughed Cass. She got a kick out of the way her friends continued to call him doctor no matter what. "And he's amazing. He's meeting us here, should be any minute now." She'd seen him every weekend since November. Either she went to Burlington, or he visited Montreal. But tonight, she had some special news.

The gathering was casual and low key; close friends and family only. Zeb had texted to say he was running late, and would miss the eight o'clock ceremony.

He finally arrived, apologizing for his tardiness.

"I recognize that dress!" Zeb said, leaning in for a kiss. "You look beautiful," he whispered into her ear, remembering the last time he'd seen that dress.

"Thank you," Cass replied, recognizing the mischievous look in his eyes. "I have news," she told him.

"You do?" he was pulling her towards the dance floor, grinning. The island music was playing and their friends were dancing in the sand and laughing. "What's your news?" he was removing his shoes. He put his bare feet into the sand, grinning.

She laughed, joining him on the fake beach dance floor.

"Remember my interview?"

He nodded. He'd been overjoyed when Cass had decided to interview at a private clinic in Burlington.

"They offered me the job."

Zeb swept her off of her feet. "You're kidding me!" he said, kissing her before putting her back onto the ground. "Cassidy Novotny, will you move in with me?"

She nodded. He kissed her deeply, and then held her in his arms and started dancing. The song turned into a slow dance, and she put her head on his chest. She felt happier than she could ever remember feeling.

She couldn't wait to live with her hot doctor.

One last thing...

I would love your feedback! Please feel free to email me (gracedevon333@gmail.com) or leave a review. Also, check out Book 1 in the baily Mills Hospital series, "Her Chief Resident".

Happy reading!
Grace.

60777947R00062

Made in the USA
Lexington, KY
17 February 2017